DAN POWELL

LOOKING OUT OF BROKEN WINDOWS

SALT

CROMER

PUBLISHED BY SALT PUBLISHING

12 Norwich Road, Cromer, Norfolk NR27 0AX United Kingdom

First published by Salt Publishing, 2014

Printed and bound in the United Kingdom by Berforts Information Press Ltd

Typeset in Paperback 9.5/13

ISBN 978 1 907773 73 0 paperback

1 3 5 7 9 8 6 4 2

for Susie

The body is a house of many windows: there we all sit, showing ourselves and crying on the passers-by to come and love us.

ROBERT LOUIS STEVENSON

CONTENTS

Looking out of Broken Windows   1
Half-mown Lawn   15
Baggage   21
Demand Feeding   23
Connecting   40
Looking for Daddy   49
Strutting and Fretting   50
Leaving what's Left   52
Did You Pack this Bag Yourself?   58
What Precise Moment   71
You Might Still   73
Silhouette of a Lady   75
Soiled   77
An Unimagined Woman   85
It's a Couple of Coats Colder up There   109
Impact   111
Rubik's Cubed   112
The Bus Shelter   114
Body of Evidence   119
The Man who Lived Like a Tree   124
Things I No Longer Wish to Possess   127
Third Party, Fire & Theft   129
Ultrasound I   137
Ultrasound II   140

Ultrasound III 142
What we Don't Talk about when we Talk about Cancer 145
Storm in a Teacup 153

Acknowledgements 169

LOOKING OUT OF
BROKEN WINDOWS

Mum called to say Dad was having a baby with someone else. He'd come home from work that night, told her what he'd been up to and packed his bags. Glad of the excuse to get out of Manchester, I jumped on the last train home. I arrived a little after midnight to find all the windows dark. My door key turned in the lock but the door wouldn't open. I shoved it with my palm, then my shoulder, but still it wouldn't budge. I thumped hard on the door, imagining Mum's body sprawled on the other side.

'Mum. Mum. Open up. Mum.'

The anxiety in my voice surprised me, made me thump harder.

'Mum. Mum. Can you hear me?'

I had my fist ready to batter the door again when she appeared, wrapped in a duvet.

'Amy, what are you doing? You'll wake the street.'

'The door wouldn't open.'

She looked at me for a second, her eyebrow raised in that way she knows I hate, then, without a word, shut the door in my face.

'Nope. Fine,' she said, opening it again.

'I was worried you'd done something silly.'

'I was sleeping. Or trying to.'

She shuffled into the living room and dropped onto the sofa, huddling under the duvet. I sat beside her and she laid her head on my shoulder. I could feel her shaking.

'Oh, Mum,' I said, stroking her hair.

With the curtains closed, I didn't notice the windows until the next morning.

A web of cracks ran across the inner panes of every double glazed unit in the house. Dad's mobile kept going to voicemail so I made Mum breakfast then set about finding someone to fix the windows. I picked the last name from the Yellow Pages, Zappa Glass.

'You the homeowner?' The voice on the other end was a gravel strewn, throaty rumble.

'It's my parents' house,' I said

We agreed a time later that day and, turning to replace the receiver in its base, I found Mum, in her pyjamas, watching me.

'Who're you calling?'

'Just a glazier.'

'A what?'

'Someone to fix the windows.'

She walked to the bay window of the front room, inspected the glass.

'What's wrong with them?'

'They're all broken. What happened last night?'

'What are you talking about?' She turned to face me, her confusion hardening into concern.

'The windows, Mum. The inside panes of the double-glazing, they're cracked. All of them.'

She followed a fracture line in the centre pane of the bay with her finger. I could see she didn't see it, though.

For her, the glass remained smooth and hard and unbroken.

'Don't be silly, love,' she said. She leaned in, kissed my cheek. 'So nice to have you home. I'm going for a bath.'

I didn't move, just stared at the cracks. Her footsteps up the stairs and across the landing were replaced, in time, with the banging of pipes and the rush of water.

The glazier's ancient Transit was the colour of rust, the words *I Will Try To Fix You* running in faded paint under the Zappa Glass logo. He wore dirty blue overalls with the logo embroidered on the left breast, the top buttons open, a thick tangle of dark chest hair bursting through the gap. The hair upon his head sprouted long and thick, like fur, and a dense beard filled his face, alert dark eyes peering out as if over a hedge. He clamped a chewed pencil in the fierce vice of his teeth, the end splintered, its charcoal vein exposed.

'You called about your windows?' he said around the pencil, the bass rumble of his voice felt as much as heard.

He wrapped a calloused hand around my own, his handshake like a hug.

'Mike Zappa, Zappa Glass. I see the problem's as you said.'

He nodded to the bay window. In the stark early morning sun, the whole and unbroken outer panes reflected their shattered twins.

'Amy, who is that?'

Mum stood on the stairs in her robe, her hair wrapped in a towel. Before I could answer, the glazier stepped round me with surprising grace and crossed the hall to meet Mum coming down. She stopped a step or two from the bottom of the stairs and pulled her robe tighter about herself.

'Mike Zappa,' he said, taking her hand. His furry arms sprouted from the rolled sleeves of his overalls, his large feet were heavily booted, tufts of hair burst up from his open collar and his muscles rippled as he moved. With his beard and hair these things worked to create the impression of not a man so much as a bear in clothes. 'And this must be your sister?'

Mum giggled as he kissed the back of her hand, his fat lips puckered and pink within the grizzle of his beard.

'This is my mum. It's her house. Mum, Mr Zappa's going to fix the windows.'

'There's nothing wrong with the windows.'

'I'll be the judge of that.' Mike Zappa led Mum off the stairs, began to guide her down the hall to the kitchen. 'Why don't you stick the kettle on and let me worry about the windows.'

I waited for Mum to argue but she just nodded and smiled and asked him how he liked his tea.

'Milky and sweet, like my women,' he said, his laugh a landslide.

Mum giggled back and trotted into the kitchen. His tongue flickered to his lips as he turned to me and grinned. 'Take me to your windows.'

I showed him to the patio units, where he stood unmoving for a moment before opening his arms out wide. He sucked in a lengthy breath and held it. His arms seemed to measure the span of the doors exactly, and then, slowly, he brought his hands together, exhaling in a long loud burst.

'They're all like this?' He ran a fingertip back and forth over one of the cracks.

'Just the interior panes.'

'And your mum doesn't see anything wrong with them?'

I nodded.

Beginning at the top of the sliding door, he traced the largest crack running down the otherwise smooth surface with his thick index finger, the action leaving him in a crouch.

'As I thought.' He looked up from his squatting position, as if preparing to pounce. 'It's a good thing you called me.'

He sprang up from the base of the patio windows and raced upstairs. I followed and found him stretched over the bathroom sink, his gut resting on the edge, tapping a finger against the cracked pane in the unit above the sink.

'Exactly as I thought.'

'I'm sorry, what?'

He turned from the window, his wild grin bright within the black of his beard.

'The spontaneous, simultaneous and specific nature of the damage, the fact you and I see it and your mother doesn't, all points to one thing.' Mike Zappa paused. With the mauled pencil he jotted something on a scrap of paper pulled from the pocket of his shirt, folded the paper and stuffed it away again. 'A textbook case of the metaphorical breaking of literal windows.' He sucked air through his teeth in that way tradesmen do. 'Fixing this type of damage, to this number of windows, well, sorry love, that's going to cost.' He stuffed the pencil back in his mouth, gnawing the end and nodding to himself. 'Yes, yes, yes. Going to take something special to fix this.'

'I'm sorry, a metaphorical what?' I started to say, but he was already on the move again.

'I should think that tea your mother promised is ready.'

~

Downstairs he measured the kitchen windows.

'Here you go.' Mum held Dad's *World's Greatest Lover* mug out for him. He snapped his measuring tape back into its casing and took the mug from her, his hands brushing hers. He read the words on the mug with a grin then swigged his tea.

'Ahhhhhhhhh.' He wiped his beard with the back of his hand. 'Perfect splash, that.'

I swear Mum blushed.

'May I ask how old these units are?'

'They were put in just after we moved in. I was pregnant, so that'd be almost twenty years ago now.'

'Windows that age, it's a good idea to have remedial work done from time to time to ensure longevity,' Mike Zappa said. 'Don't worry. I'll make it so these windows last another twenty years.' He winked at Mum.

'My adulterous husband's paying, so you go right ahead, Mr Zappa.' Mum was batting her lashes.

'Shouldn't you be getting dressed?' I widened my eyes at her but she ignored me.

'I'm talking to Mr Zappa.' She moved closer to him, pushed her chest forward, her cleavage rising within her robe, her skin still damp from her shower.

Mike Zappa ran his eyes over Mum's chest. 'Please, call me Mike.'

'Jennifer.'

'Lovely name,' he said and she giggled again.

Mum got out the biscuits and Mike Zappa crunched his way through half a packet of custard creams before getting up to finish measuring the rest of the windows. He said he'd be in touch in a day or so with a quote.

'Be seeing you, Jennifer,' he called to Mum, turning and winking from the garden gate.

I watched her cheeks flush and she waved, a girlish flick of a thing.

'Bloody hell, Mum.'

'What?'

I left her watching Mike Zappa's van scream up the road.

I called another glazier for a second opinion, this time picking the most mundane sounding firm, Smith and Son. A thin man with thick glasses came out that afternoon but was quickly irritated. As far as he could see, there was nothing wrong with the windows.

That night Mum and I ate pizza in front of the TV, watching some reality-show tragedy play out. We finished the only bottle of wine in the house quickly so I grabbed my coat and headed out for more. The off-licence was just round the block in the small row of shops down from my old primary school. I bought the cheapest Shiraz they had, and a bar of Dairy Milk. The plan was to put on a DVD, relax and forget about Dad and the windows and everything.

Back at the house, again the front door refused to open. I pushed, shouldered, even kicked at it, but the door remained firmly closed. I knew the back door would likely be unlocked so I nipped round the side. The light from the kitchen projected the window fractures onto the brick paved patio. The handle of the back door turned, but the door stayed jammed in the frame. Giving up I tapped the glass to get Mum's attention.

'What're you playing at?'

'I couldn't open the front door again. This one either.'

I waited for the raised eyebrow.

'Call that nice Mr Zappa, perhaps he knows what's going on,' she said instead.

I called the next morning and explained about the doors. Mike Zappa offered to consult a friend in the trade.

'He works with ideas of wood, conceptual timber, that sort of thing. If there's a problem with your doors, he'll sort you out.' He sounded like he was chewing on the pencil as he spoke. 'You the only one experiencing the problem with the doors?'

'Yes.'

He sucked air in through his teeth.

'I'll see what he says. As for your windows, you've two options. You can employ what we in the trade call the metaphorical fix, where we, the qualified profession- als, engage in repairs just as we would a literal, physical problem, only with metaphorical materials. These are considerably more expensive than more readily-available literal ones of course.'

'And option two?'

'I could do a bodge job and replace the damaged panes with new standard ones, but that'd be false economy. They'd only go again a few weeks down the line. Meta- phorically broken windows need to be fixed right to have the job last.'

The line crackled with the rustling of paper and a scratching sound.

'Fifteen hundred quid should cover a proper job. Half up front for materials and whatnot.'

'That seems a lot to fix damage you say doesn't really exist.'

Another suck of air, this one much bigger.

'Don't misunderstand me, metaphorical damage is

very real. We have to manufacture most of the materials ourselves; each batch is job-specific. We're talking materials reinforced with meaning, materials that won't buckle under scrutiny, that can withstand criticism.'

More rustling of paper, more scratching.

'The cheapest I could start for is five hundred, take it or leave it.'

'I'll have to check with my parents, it's their house, after all.'

'No drama.' I swear I heard him grin. 'Call soon though, work's always coming in. You don't want to be stuck once we're busy elsewhere.'

I called Dad at work.

'Now's not a good time.'

'It never is. When are you coming home?'

'I'm not.'

We both listened to silence while I waited for him to explain.

'I'm missing classes,' I said, buckling.

'So go back to Manchester.'

'I'm not sure Mum can be left.'

'She can. I left her.'

'Why?'

'I've met someone, she's having a baby.'

'I meant, why are you doing that? Why are you starting all over again? Why now?'

'Ask your mother.'

'She won't talk about it.'

'There you go then.'

'What?'

'Let her be. Go back to Manchester. She'll sort herself out, she'll have to.'

'Jesus, Dad, that's a bit harsh.'

'Yes, it is, but there you go.'

'There's a problem with the house, too.'

'What problem?'

I told him about the windows and Mike Zappa.

'I don't know what to do with it all, Dad. It sounds like bullshit. Just not sure whether it's Mum's or the glazier's.'

'Nice try.'

'Pardon?'

'As a reason for getting me home, I have to say it's inventive.'

'She's flirting with him. It's very sad.'

'I'm sure it is. Good for her.'

Laughing, he put the phone down.

Over a thrown-together dinner of pasta and chicken, I tried again with Mum.

'They're broken, all of them.' I pointed to the cracks through the two large panes of the unit over the kitchen sink.

'Love, there's nothing wrong with them.'

I topped up our wine glasses.

'Why did Dad leave?'

'Ask him.'

'He told me to ask you.'

'There you are then.'

She took a swig of wine and smiled.

'Jesus, you two are as bad as each other. Call yourself bloody adults.'

Mum didn't say anything.

'Alright. Forget it. None of my business. You two sort it out. Just tell me what you're going to do about the windows.'

'There's nothing wrong with the windows.'

I knocked back my wine then collected up the dirty plates, scraping the leftovers into a pile of half-eaten mush. 'Fine. If there's no problem then there's no need for me to be here.' I flicked the food into the bin, clattered the plates into the dishwasher.

'I didn't ask you to come home.'

'You didn't say the words, but that's exactly what you did.'

'Well, you can go now.'

Mum wasn't angry as she said this. She stepped over to where I had started washing-up the big pan and rested her head between my shoulders, her arms wrapped round my waist.

'I'll be okay,' she said. 'These things happen.'

'These things happen?'

'Yes,' she said, 'These things do.'

I decided to hang around one more day before going back to Uni, just to be sure. By the time I woke on Friday morning, Mum was already up and out of the house. I left Mike Zappa a message explaining we wouldn't be bothering with the repairs then headed into town to do some shopping.

It was late afternoon by the time I got back. I could hear hushed voices and a tapping sound coming from upstairs.

'Mum, you home?' I called.

Sitting on the stairs to take off my shoes, I saw the work boots: dark brown with heavy rubber soles, one upright, the other laying on its side. I heard someone laughing.

'Mum?' I called.

I climbed the stairs and crossed to her bedroom door.

11

The noise had stopped. Before I could knock, the door opened to reveal a naked Mike Zappa, even more bear-like without clothes, holding a glutted and sagging condom over the end of his wilted penis.

''Scuse me,' he said and stepped lightly past me and into the bathroom, locking the door behind him.

I took a single step into my mother's room. A musky animal smell hung in the air. She lay, covered in the duvet, her face flushed.

'Jesus, Mum.'

'These things happen,' she said and smiled the first real smile I had seen on her face since coming home.

Only then, struggling with the image of the shriveled cock and wrinkled condom dangling beneath the globed bulk of Mike Zappa's belly, did I realise I had let myself in with my key and that the windows, all the windows, were no longer broken.

Mike Zappa came downstairs in his overalls as I was calling for a taxi to take me to the station. He sat on the stairs, his hair slicked back, a damp fur smell rising from him.

'It appears the fix was easier than I thought,' he said, pulling on his boots. 'Don't fret, they'll be no charge for, shall we say, services rendered.'

I rolled my eyes and pointed with my free hand at the phone still ringing and ringing in my ear.

'I'll be off then,' he said.

His van could still be heard screaming up the road when, finally, someone at the taxi firm picked up.

'ABC, where to?'

I didn't answer. The voice on the other end repeated the question but I remained at a loss.

~

Back in Manchester, I decided to surprise Rich. We'd been seeing each other since Freshers' Week, had even spent Christmas together at his parents'. He hadn't met mine yet. I got myself buzzed into his hall of residence and knocked on his door. There was no answer so I checked the shared spaces of the living room and kitchen but no one had seen him since lunch. It was after five.

I tapped *Whr r u?* into my phone.

I got a can of Coke from the vending machine in the lobby of the Halls, drank it, then called him.

'I'm back, where are you?'

'The library. Catching up on some work.'

'Who are you and what have you done with my boy-friend?'

I thought I heard laughter in the background.

'What was that?'

'Nothing. Look, can I call you later?'

Again I heard laughter, quiet but definitely there, where he was. Filtered as it was through the phone, I couldn't tell whether the laughter was quiet and close to Rich or loud but further away.

'Is someone there with you?'

'I'm in the library, there's a lot of people here with me.'

I listened for the laugh, but it didn't come again.

'Look, I'll be here a while. I'll call you when I get out,' Rich said and hung up.

I walked back to my shared house. The girls were getting ready to go clubbing. I said I needed an early night and went to my room to unpack. Once they left I stuck a frozen pizza on and took the remains of the wine they'd opened back up to my room. I finished the bottle, half-watching the end of *Hollyoaks*, my phone beside me, then I slumped back on the bed.

I thought about checking the pizza. I thought about getting more wine. I thought about Mum and Dad. I tried to remember exactly what the laughter on the phone had sounded like. The ceiling, empty except for the light fitting, stared at me. Staring back, I watched cracks emerge from the plastic cup of the ceiling rose and spread across the magnolia expanse, reaching for where the walls met the ceiling.

HALF-MOWN LAWN

Annie is ready for an empty house by the time everyone has finally gone home. She spends the first hour or so flitting from room to room, straightening cushions and rescuing the odd missed wine glass from the bookshelves upstairs, before ending up in her rocking chair staring out the bedroom window as frail white clouds sidle past.

Below, the long grass of the half-mown lawn shivers in the wind, the mower still stood at the checkpoint between the cut and uncut. Where the grass is short, blades poke from the soil like a crew cut. The shape pressed into the long grass calls for her attention, but she refuses its demands.

At the kitchen table, Annie tears a piece of paper from a message pad. She writes the name of the local store at the top. Underneath she writes headings: *Frozen*, *Fresh*, *Dairy*, *Fruit/Veg*, *Household*. Underneath each she creates columns of her needs, organising *oven-chips*, *apples*, *sponge scourers* and *skimmed milk* into manageable groups. Under the heading *Fresh* she writes *whole chicken*. The words hold her for a moment before she crosses them through with a single line and writes *chicken breast* in the space beneath. She stands in the pantry, waiting for the empty spaces on the shelves to reveal what is missing from her list. The gaps between the pickle jars, rows of cereal boxes and tinned goods are indecipherable, redacted text that she cannot make sense of. Back at the table she turns over her paper and makes another list. On it she writes,

Things I will miss:
Him polishing his shoes every morning
The way he looked in a suit
His mixing five different types of cereal for breakfast
The quiet knock of his briefcase on the hall floor
The sound of his breath, warm on my back at four in the
morning

She continues like this until long past the local shop's closing time; resigns herself to driving to the all-night Tesco.

In the aisles, Annie searches for the items on her list, filling her trolley with washing-up liquid, onions, bread and those biscuits he liked. As each item drops into the trolley, she crosses a list entry out with an Ikea pencil found in her coat pocket. She flips the list to check the back and finds herself staring at the things she will miss. Her eyes flick up at the signs hanging from the false ceiling of the supermarket, as if simply by looking she will find the section he is hiding in.

At the checkout she places her shopping on the conveyor, slotting a customer divider directly behind her things. Her items move slowly towards the till and she rearranges them, grouping together the fruit and vegetables, the dairy, the household goods. The checkout girl swipes the shopping through in a flurry of bleeps and Annie struggles to keep pace as she fills up her bags for life.

'£57.81,' says the checkout girl.

Annie rummages in her handbag.

'I seem to have left my purse at home,' she says.

The checkout girl huffs, then hits the button next to the till to call a supervisor.

'It's my first day. I don't know what to do about this,' she says.

'I don't know what to do either,' Annie says, her eyes checking the aisle signs once more.

Annie takes two eggs, a slice of ham, the cheese and the last of the tomatoes from the fridge. The oil warming in her small omelette pan, she cracks the eggs into a cup and scrambles the yolks with a fork. The ham and tomato sit in chopped piles beside a mound of grated cheddar.

The puddle of oil spreads across the frying pan, seeking the heat, and she waits until it is ready before pouring out the eggs. She sprinkles ham, then tomato, then cheese, letting each sink into the surface of the egg before adding the next. Once finished, she deposits the omelette onto a clean plate, leaving the pan and chopping board beside the cooling hob.

On the table a single space is laid and she empties the remains of a bottle of red into her wine glass. She takes her time with the meal, slicing small mouthfuls from the omelette, her wine sitting untouched beside her plate. In this way she avoids the kitchen window.

Paul, Jenny and the grandkids stayed behind after friends and family had gone home. Jenny busied herself, stacking the glasses and plates into the dishwasher.

'I could mow the lawn for you, Mum,' Paul said.

'Don't you fucking touch it!' Annie heard herself scream.

A beat of silence followed before the children whispered 'Granny did a swear' and Jenny ushered them into the kitchen for ice-cream. Flushed, Annie collapsed into an armchair but didn't cry.

'It's okay, Mum,' Paul told her. But it wasn't.

Now Annie picks up the phone and dials his number.

'Mum?' he says, 'is everything okay? Do you need me to come over?'

'Can you mow the lawn tomorrow?' is all she says.

'Of course. You're sure?'

She presses the *end call* button without replying.

Annie removes the dirty dishes from the dishwasher and places them in order upon the work surface before turning on both taps. The sink fills quickly and she takes each item from the pile and scrubs them in the soapy water. The caked-on stains of the Pyrex dishes take time and elbow grease to remove. Twice she empties the sink, replacing the brown, greasy water with fresh suds.

The draining board is soon crammed and she pulls a clean tea towel from the drawer. Each item is dried and tucked away in the kitchen cupboards, one at a time, even the cutlery, before she refills the sink a third time and sets about the final pile of dirty crockery. Only now, with the garden growing indistinct in the dusk, does Annie look out through the kitchen window at the dimming outline of the shape in the grass, her hands continuing to scrub at food stains already removed.

Annie shuts off the lights in the front room and takes her book and a cup of jasmine tea upstairs. She sits in the rocking chair, her book on her lap, and lets her tea grow cold. When, finally, she looks down at the shape in the grass, it is barely visible in the dim light provided by the nearby street lamps.

Only days ago, though it already feels much longer, she sat in the rocker by the window, reading, as he started the job. She had smiled, glancing down at him mowing the lawn, before losing herself in her book. It was the sound of the mower shutting off, too soon for him to have finished, that pulled her from her reading. When he turned to look up at the window, she saw it in his face. He crumpled onto the lawn as she rose from her chair.

Annie flosses, careful to run the white thread deep below the gum line where plaque forms, just as the hygienist showed her. She brushes her teeth for the full two minutes. In the mirror her mouth fills with toothpaste foam until she has to spit. A quick cold-water rinse, then she switches off the en-suite light and closes the door behind her.

Their double bed has fresh sheets; probably Jenny being helpful. Annie climbs in her side of the bed, lies facing where he should be. There is no indentation or crease in the bottom sheet or pillow on his side, any trace of him smoothed out when the sheets were replaced. She scoots over and buries her face in his pillow, but it is the smell of detergent that fills her nostrils.

Unable to sleep, Annie pulls her dressing gown about her, walks downstairs, slips on her garden shoes and steps slowly out, taking care only to walk on the mown part of the lawn. The summer night air is warm, even for the time of year. Where he fell, the shape of him remains pressed in the long grass.

Annie crouches and runs her finger around his outline, the compacted grass inside like a crop circle in the shape of a man. She strokes where his cheek pressed to the ground, almost sees his face bristling with irritation as it did the morning she complained about the unmown lawn.

Without looking around, she climbs into the outline of him and lays down, careful to keep herself entirely within its boundaries. She gently places her head on his broad chest, spooning her legs onto his, just as she used to when they were younger. The smell of cut grass is an embrace now, where, in the hospital, kissing the fingers of his cooling hands, it had overwhelmed her. Annie lies still and listens for his heartbeat.

BAGGAGE

1

Buying the leather sample bag, he made doubly sure it was large enough to hold every one of his smiles. Happy with his selection, he clicked the twin clasps shut, twirled the miniature combination locks, and imagined capturing every last one within the plush interior.

The woman behind the counter advised him that the bag came with a twenty-four month guarantee covering stitching and handles.

'I'll keep my receipt,' he said, a polite smile finding its way to his lips. He made a mental note to place that one deep inside the bag's lowest pockets when he got home.

Leaving the shop, he thought of the evening ahead, glass of wine on the coffee table, placing his smiles, one by one, inside the soft lining of the leather sample bag. A grin of pleasure played across his lips. He would be sure to shut that one away last.

2

He soon returned to the shop asking for a bag of the exact same make and size. That was important.

The woman behind the counter was concerned that the

other had failed in some way, but he assured her that the only reason he required another was because he was so pleased with the first.

'The volume and shape of this particular style sample bag is perfect for my needs,' he said. He did not smile this visit. He had left his smiles at home, safely fastened away behind the twin clasps of his first purchase.

Leaving the shop, his thoughts brimmed once more with visions of filling the soft lining of the sample bag, this time with his frowns. He would bag them up to save himself the bother. Thinking of completion, sadness flickered across his features, and he realised he would have to return to the shop for another bag. If he still could, he would have smiled.

3

In time, as his finances and his self-awareness allowed, he purchased a bag for each distinct emotional expression. Leather sample bags weren't cheap, and often he found an emotion not previously packed away sneak up on him.

He placed each bag on a shelf in his bedroom closet, a room-sized space he could have easily converted to an en-suite if he had felt the need for one. Having filled seventeen bags, he was sure, this time, that he was finished.

He checked his face in the mirror hung on the back of the closet door. A perfect blank stared back, unmoving, giving away nothing. Relief blasted from the neurons of his traitorous brain to his nervous system, flooding his face with movement, sagging his jaw, loosening his eyes, exhaling his lungs, filling his cheeks with air.

He cursed twice to himself and counted the days to payday.

DEMAND FEEDING

Chris keeps a box of man-size tissues by the bed. On nights we don't have sex, the pulse of his tugging shakes the mattress and wakes me. I don't speak, just lie still, desperate to get back off to sleep, knowing that Andy will wake for his feed soon. Thankfully it never takes Chris long to finish. There is a final scuffle under the covers as he catches his cum and wipes himself, dumping the sticky tissues under the bed.

We don't talk about this.

Another thing we don't talk about is how Adam, as if unsatisfied at the end of each feed, clamps my nipple in his gums and bites. At first my pained yelping would spook him into letting go, or I would yank him from my breast without thinking, tearing and scraping my nipple. Now, when he does this, I slip my little finger between gum and nipple and prise him off, just like my midwife showed me. He falls asleep on my lap then, his soft face blurred with satisfaction. This is just part of the routine, like shitty nappies or waking to the sound of wailing at three in the morning.

Before trying for a baby, our sex life had already reached something of a plateau: less than a handful of positions, ribbed condoms for special occasions, the odd bit of oral sex; all of it usually taking place the night before I washed the sheets. Chris tried his best to spice things up: buying nice underwear, booking spontaneous meals out, organising weekends away. I told him it wasn't him, it was me. That all marriages go through this.

'There's an ebb and flow,' I said.

'I'm sick of the ebb,' he said, 'I'm tired of waiting for the flow.'

Sometimes I think he only agreed to try for a baby because he realised it meant regular sex, at least for a while. Plus he got to ditch the condoms. I suffered the full list of side-effects whenever I tried the pill: headaches, nausea, painfully tender breasts, and of course, the weight gain. In the end I saved myself the deep vein thrombosis, heart attack or stroke. Condoms, if a little inconvenient and unsexy, were at least side-effect-free.

For Chris, not having to rely on a condom meant we were free to do it wherever and whenever we liked. Which he insisted we did. We started on the sofa, cuddled-up, watching TV in our underwear, quickies in the advert breaks, then off to the kitchen for snacks and tea before starting again. In the kitchen itself, stood at the sink, Chris behind me, a zipless fuck with my skirt raised, neighbours walking past the window, oblivious. Chris on his back on the lawn, me astride him, the fall of my summer dress long enough to cover where our bodies met. I'd never had sex in a car, so he made sure we fixed that too. We even nipped into the park one night on the way back from the pub and shagged on the bandstand like teenagers.

I plotted my cycle, noting down days and times and temperatures, keeping track of my ovulation with a notebook and an Excel spreadsheet. Chris laughed at my sex rota, but kept at it, always eager, hurrying home on those days when my falling pregnant was most likely, while I watched and waited for the first sign, any sign, I might be pregnant. But, for all our rigorous and conscientious focus on the task at hand, for all our fucking, the baby did not come.

Andy's cries drag me from my bed. The letdown washing through me makes me ache. He wriggles in my arms, rooting for my nipple, latching quickly, his mouth open wide, lips flared, his chin and nose pressed to my breast so that in profile I see the Special K flourish his lips make. The steady tug of him is like a heartbeat we share, and I lay my head back on a cushion and close my eyes and the early nights of sore nipples, when we struggled together, Andy and I, to get him to latch properly, when I obsessed over helping him make that Special K shape, those nights when I would grind my teeth at the pain, jaw aching and clicking in time to his sucking, those nights seem far away now.

My right breast empty, I swap him to the left and feel the ache again as he draws my milk to him. I doze as he drains me. It is then, both breasts empty and me half asleep, that his tiny mouth snaps shut. I stifle my yell, force it through my teeth as a gasp, as my finger slides between his lips to lever him off. I place him on my lap and inspect my nipple but can see nothing in the dark. I press a clean nursing pad to it and hoist it back into my maternity bra, struggling one-handed with the clasp, the other resting on Andy's belly to keep him from rolling off my lap. He is already sleeping. I place him in his cot and he rolls to his front, shuffles his bum into the air. I watch him for a moment, massaging my breast with my palm.

Back in bed I pull the duvet over me, still listening for Andy, not wanting to drift back to sleep until I am sure he has settled. My breast throbs and the backache I've carried around since before Andy was born flares up as I try to get comfortable. I feel Chris roll to face me, his hand slipping to my belly, sliding to my breast.

'Not now,' I whisper.

I feel his breath huff against my cheek.

'Fuck sake,' he says and rolls back over to his side.

I am on the edge of sleep when I feel the mattress begin to throb.

No one imagines not getting pregnant. When you decide to have a baby your head fills with thoughts of morning sickness, getting fat, labour and, most of all, the end product, a brand new person you will love no matter what. On a more practical level you start to think about moving to a place with more rooms, decorating a nursery, trading the sporty hatchback for a family car. You think about all the things that have to change before baby comes. No one thinks about baby not coming. No one thinks about baby not coming, until baby doesn't come.

When baby doesn't come, you think about blame. You hope it isn't you, don't want it to be your reproductive system letting the side down, but neither do you want it to be his. You love him enough to not want him to feel like less of a man, even as you don't want to be told you are less of a woman. You want things to be simple, solved with a pill or a hormone injection or eating more fruit. The failure of your bodies, his and your own, to function properly frustrates you as if they were faulty home appliances. These things should just work. So you get someone in to have a look and see what's wrong.

But before you can do that you have to have the conversation. Really a series of conversations, all about the same thing, each subsequent one picking up where the last left off; all of a piece, but chopped-up to fit around everything else you've got going on. You talk a little in the morning, but have to cut it short or be late for work. You arrive home late, or he does, too tired to talk about it. By the time the weekend arrives you're both too tightly wound from thinking about it separately, and your ideas have fixed so solidly in the time you've spent thinking about it alone that seeing where the other is coming from becomes impossible.

'We need to find out what's wrong,' you say.

'What if it's just not the right time?' he says.

'My clock's ticking,' you say.

'It just feels weird,' he says.

'You leave enough of the stuff on tissues under the bed, what's the difference?'

'It's like taking an exam,' he says.

'Let's just keep trying,' he says.

'Just for a bit,' he says.

Only the sex has ground to a halt. You can't help thinking that it's all for nothing. You associate sex too much with failure and he reads your coldness as coldness to him and he rolls over and turns his back and you can't bring yourself to cross the bed and reassure him because you need him to reassure you. You need him to want a baby. You need him to want to try everything to make sure it happens. Most of all, you need him to wank into a sample cup instead of a wad of tissues.

Andy wakes early, crying to be fed again. I take him downstairs. It is still dark outside. He devours both breasts again, but I pull him away before he has chance to bite. I lay him at my feet for a moment and check my breast. There is blood on the nursing pad when I remove it, a dark brown stain on the white. The cut is on the dark skin of the areola. I leave Andy to wriggle on the floor for a moment while I root through the nappy sacks, spare vests and packs of wipes jammed into the baby bag and pull out my cream. I rub some into both nipples and think about changing my bra, but decide to wait till I have chance to shower.

I carry Andy to the kitchen and put the kettle on. He coos at me, arms flailing to reach my face. I kiss his forehead then stare out the kitchen window into the dark garden beyond. Our reflection on the glass blocks the view, the ticking kitchen strip-light making it hard to see outside. There have been many nights like this since Andy was born, the two of us awake while Chris sleeps upstairs. The novelty of the first couple of nights' tea and toast together at two a.m. wore off quickly for him. Now the nights blur into one long stretch, punctuated by stolen minutes of sleep. During the day, the outside world hovers beyond the windows like a back projection or a memory of somewhere I used to live.

I put Andy down on his play mat and lie on the sofa watching him. He wriggles but is a long way from being able to roll himself over yet. I doze for a while, opening my eyes when I hear Chris in the kitchen.

'Tea?' he calls.

He brings me a mug and we sit together on the sofa. Andy swings his hands up at a plush bumblebee hanging from the arch of his play mat. His fingers brush it and he squeals.

'Bad night?' Chris holds his mug in front of him.

'The usual. Sorry if I was short with you. He bit me while he was feeding.'

Chris doesn't answer for a moment, and when he does he just says, 'Don't worry about it.'

He gets up from the sofa with a sigh and crouches next

to Andy, holds out a finger and lets him wrap a pudgy fist around it.

'See you later, little man,' he says then stands. 'I better get to work.'

I nod and he leaves.

Once Chris agreed to provide a sample, the preliminary tests got as far as checking his sperm.

'You have a low count, I'm afraid,' the doctor said.

'Must be some mistake,' Chris said.

'What can we do?' I said.

The doctor ran through possible causes, but Chris hadn't suffered a testicular injury, wasn't malnourished, didn't take regular saunas or hot tubs, had quit smoking years ago, had never taken cocaine or smoked marijuana, was taking no prescription medications, had not to his knowledge been exposed to environmental toxins, radiation or heavy metals, was not obese, under stress or undertaking excessive physical or mental exertion, nor was he a keen cyclist.

'Cyclist?' I said.

'Blood vessels and nerves can be damaged due to pressure from the bike seat over long periods.' The doctor turned to Chris. 'How often do you ejaculate within a given week?'

'The usual amount,' Chris said.

'A lot,' I said at the same time.

The doctor looked from Chris to me and back again.

'A lot,' Chris said, reddening.

'Maintain a gap of three to four days between ejaculations, avoid tight underwear, hot tubs and anything else that might increase the temperature of the testicles.' The doctor handed Chris another plastic tub. 'Wait three or four days then bring another sample.'

Carol, the Health Visitor, arrives after Chris has left for work. She asks if I am still taking my vitamins. I am. She weighs Andy. As she plots a point on the graph in his red book, her brow furrows, her lips pull down a little.

'He's beginning to display a negative trend,' Carol says and shows me the chart. Andy's line arcs lower the further from birth it goes, curving downwards where the projected lines printed on the sheet stretch up and across and off the page. 'It may be he's not feeding long enough, only getting fore milk.'

I tell her I feed on demand as she has advised. I tell her he drains both breasts before he's finished.

Carol lifts Andy from the scales, refits his nappy. 'You may need to supplement his breast feeds with formula,' she says, her eyes on Andy.

I feel the tears drip from my cheeks before I realise I am crying. Carol puts Andy on his play mat, sits down beside me and puts an arm round my shoulders. She tells me not to worry. She tells me to buy a steriliser and bottles and formula. She tells me to have Andy weighed at the clinic in a week's time. She tells me we'll see how things are in a couple of weeks. Again, she tells me not to worry.

When Chris got home on the third day, he practically pounced on me.

'The doctor said four days.' I pushed him away, turned to put the kettle on.

'He said three or four.' Chris pressed himself up behind me, sliding his arms under mine, his hands cupping my breasts. 'C'mon.'

Uncoupling his hands, I wriggled from his grasp.

'Four,' I said. 'And the doctor said to save it for a sample, not sex.'

'Surely all that stocked-up sperm would be better used having a crack at getting you pregnant than swimming in a jar.'

'Four days and a sample, that's what we were told, that's what you're doing.' I folded my arms, the mugs of tea steaming and stewing behind me. 'Now, do you want your tea?'

'Don't bother yourself, I'm going for a shower,' Chris said, and stomped up the stairs.

'No wanking,' I called after him. He slammed the bathroom door in reply.

I left the jar on his bedside table for when he woke the next morning. He left without having breakfast or saying goodbye. I found the jar where Chris left it. The turbid gloop slopped inside gave no indication of virility, no sign of motility. It displayed all the potential of wallpaper paste.

When I try to talk to Chris about supplementing feeds, I am where I always seem to be, in the armchair, Andy guzzling at my breast.

'What do you think?' I say.

'What does the Health Visitor say you should do?' A half-chewed mouthful of toast mushes his words as he stands in the kitchen doorway.

'I've already told you,' I say and then tell him again.

'Do that,' he says.

'But the books say not to mix the two,' I say.

'Oh fuck, not the books again.' He rolls his eyes.

I mentioned the books yesterday, when he asked again about sex.

'Look, do what you think. Do bottles and breast if you

want. I'll do the bottle feeds if you want, just please shut up about the bloody books.'

'You're not still pissed off about that?'

'It's been longer than six weeks.'

'Can we please not talk about this now?'

'Great, so now we can't even talk about it?'

'We can talk about it, just not now, now we're talking about something else, something important to me.'

'So our sex life isn't important to you?'

'I didn't say that. You're putting words in my mouth. I just need your help.'

'So fuck what I need?'

I don't get chance to answer. While we've been talking Andy's drained the breast and he bites down. I scream, jabbing my finger in his mouth to pry him off.

'Fuck. Fuck. Fuck,' I say and Andy begins to bawl. I pull him to me.

'Do I look like someone thinking about sex?' I say to Chris, but he is staring at my still-exposed breast, the enflamed nipple.

'Jesus Chris,' I say.

Chris looks at Andy, then back at me. His eyes remind me of the day Andy was born.

'You know how difficult the birth was,' I say. 'You think I feel like throwing my legs in the air after all that. If you need sex that badly perhaps you should fuck off and get it somewhere else.'

My voice is shrill in my ears. Chris doesn't say anything.

'I'm not ready,' I say, bringing my voice down.

'You're going to have to wait,' I say.

'The books say the six week thing is a myth,' I say.

'Oh fuck the books,' he says.

He doesn't leave though. Today is Saturday. We

are going out to look at beds in the hope it will help with my back. Today he just takes his toast back to the kitchen. Later, the saleswoman in the store suggests buying two single mattresses for the frame instead of a king.

'A traditional king will suffer mid-mattress dipping under the weight of two people, creating a valley of insufficient support. Worst cases cause sleepers to roll together into the dip.' To illustrate, the saleswoman laces her fingers together to form a shallow v-shape. 'Individual mattresses provide superior support,' she says, unhooking her hands and holding them side-by-side, palms up, dead level.

'It's the first step towards separate beds,' is all Chris says in the car on the way home.

The sperm count of the four-day sample was much improved.

'Plan your intercourse around your ovulation, and keep at least four days between ejaculations to ensure more viable sperm counts,' the doctor said.

I plotted my cycle on a chart, worked out my most fertile days, worked in Chris's four-day recuperations, then emailed Chris a copy. I allowed him more than one go at things. I figured a few extra samples along with the super-sample wouldn't hurt and Chris didn't argue. He saved the arguing for the four-day dry spell.

Two months later I was pregnant. Morning sickness kicked in something terrible and hung around. I was off sex again and Chris stopped asking after the first few rejections. The pregnancy rattled along without anything out of the ordinary, if you can call walking round with a whole other person inside you ordinary. Chris put in overtime while I put on weight.

'I've been reading about pregnancy sex,' Chris said one night in my sixth month.

I was lying across the sofa with my head on his belly. Things were feeling nice, relaxed. Until he said that. I pretended not to hear, letting *Location Location* fill the silence around us, Kirsty and Phil showing some sad-looking couple round an even sadder-looking detached house with outbuildings.

'It's suffering a bit from neglect, but a little attention could have it feeling better in no time,' Kirsty told the nodding couple.

Chris snorted and stood up, letting my head drop back onto the sofa cushions.

'I'm going for a shower,' he said.

They say sleep when the baby sleeps, so you feed baby, put him in the Moses basket beside the bed and lie there, curtains drawn, and sleep until he wakes. That maybe works for the first couple of weeks when hubby is on paternity and doing his best to be involved, even if that really only means cooking the odd meal and switching on the washing machine, the tumble dryer, the dishwasher. Then hubby goes back to work and there's baby and house to think about, and other mums cope so you must too. So while baby sleeps you wash and clean and cook and iron and you get up in the night because he has to go to work. You ignore the back pain that has plagued you since the third trimester. You keep up the breast feeding, even though each feed drains you more than the last, and you look down at the baby at your breast and see something more than food being pulled from your body by those insatiable button lips.

Looking at yourself in the mirror, hair in need of a

stylist, the maternal uniform of joggers and sick-stained tee hanging off you, it's like staring at your life disappearing into the distance, the woman you were blinking out at vanishing point, leaving behind this shambles, this outline.

Then, just as you're about to lose yourself completely, you hear baby wake, only he isn't crying. Not this time. No, this time it's the soft, pillowy sound of discovery, and you sneak into the nursery and peer over the cot to find him waving his hands and cooing, and you swear the face he's pulling is a smile, that the gurgle is a laugh, and your life does blink out, does vanish, but it doesn't hurt so much because it's been replaced with this.

As with most first deliveries, my labour was long and painful and, in the end, assisted. Andy came out screaming and bloody and beautiful. So beautiful. His eyes two pools of calm water looking back at me, relaying in an instant that it had all been worth it: the sickness, the back ache, the weight gain, the exhaustion, the long labour, the pain of a slowly-healing episiotomy.

Chris was present for the birth. He held my hand, said all the right things, but I could see it in his face. If Andy's eyes were pools of calm, then Chris's were deep wells of fear. Or something else. Resentment? It was holding Andy for the first time that I watched it happen, Chris's eyes retreating, falling away, something bottomless appearing in them.

'He's beautiful,' he said, his lips, at least, smiling.

I have no idea how long Chris has been stood in the living-room doorway watching me breast feed Andy before he asks, 'Are you coming to bed soon?'

It is late. Andy woke just as Chris and I were about to go to bed.

'I won't be long. You should get to sleep.'

Chris grunts. He is staring, so I look back.

'What? I brought him down here so you could get some quiet. You've got work tomorrow.'

'Thanks for that.'

'Don't be funny.'

'I'm not being anything.'

'I'll be up as soon as I get him settled.' I nod my head at Andy.

Chris sighs.

'What?'

'You know what.'

'Not this again.'

'Yes, God forbid we should even talk about it.'

'Now? You want to talk about it now?'

'When else is there?'

Concentrating on Chris, I almost miss the signs that Andy is finishing up. I roll him gently from my nipple before he can think to bite, wipe his face with my pyjama top, then press a breast pad to my nipple.

'Just go to bed. I'll be up when I can,' I say to Chris as I tuck my breast away.

I sit Andy upon my knee, his back against my belly, and he burbles a little, waving his hands frantically at Daddy. But Daddy doesn't cross the room to take him, Daddy just stares as if uncertain how he finds himself here, as if he has slept on a train and only now wakes to find himself disembarked at the wrong station.

'Can you not just put him to bed.' Chris barely moves as he speaks. His lips break open just wide enough to let the brittle words out.

'What's it like to be jealous of your own son?' I say.

Chris snorts at this, a snarling, bitter laugh.

'Or are you just worried about where your next shag is coming from.'

'This isn't about me.'

'Bullshit, this is about you, about what you want, what you always want.'

'I've got nothing to do with this,' Chris says, waving his hand to indicate me and Andy. 'There's no space for me in this.'

'So you admit it. You admit you're jealous.'

Chris is rooted at the door. He struggles to speak for a moment, words half start, but he gives up.

'You think I'm not letting you in? Take him, then.' I hold Andy out to Chris. 'Bond with your son.'

Chris lets out a sigh and starts to cross the room.

'Don't bother if it's too much trouble.'

Pulling Andy right into me, I stomp past Chris and upstairs, hear the clumping as he takes the stairs two at a time to catch us. At the top I turn and he halts a few steps below us. Andy wriggles in my arms, grizzling. I hear my voice as if from a distance, as if this were happening next door, down the street, to someone else.

'I can only deal with one baby at a time.'

Chris doesn't say anything. But it is all there in his eyes.

'Leave us alone.'

I kick my foot at Chris's face, missing him by a fraction, but his dodging flings him back, sends him sprawling down the stairs. Andy explodes with a cheerful scream. We watch Chris roll and hit the floor, his head and back smacking the stairs over and over on the way down. He lies so still at the bottom that I think he might be dead. I hold my breath for the handful of seconds before he groans and shakes his head and pulls himself up to a sitting position. He looks up at me with those eyes. I pull Andy closer to me and turn away.

The nursery nightlight scatters primary colours and shapes across the wall. A lullaby whispers from the CD player. I sit in the rocking chair, cradle Andy, his head heavy on my breast, and we rock back and forth, back and forth, in place yet in motion.

Chris spends the night on the sofa and when I wake the next morning he is already gone.

The first time Andy bit me, he was only a few days old. We were settled in the armchair downstairs, his body bundled into mine, his face pressed to my right nipple, his chubby hand staking a claim on my left, some lifestyle channel murmuring on the TV. On automatic, my baby guzzling happily in my arms, I dozed.

Pain jolted me awake. Unable to move for a moment, my brain rattling as it haltingly attempted to assemble what was happening, I could hear someone screaming. Andy chomped harder and I realised it was my scream. The sound of it dragged the rest of me into motion and I tore him off.

Gasping, most of my breath expelled along with the scream, I surveyed my enflamed nipple. The ridge of his gums had forced a bruise red impression into the end. Andy gurned at me from where he lay on my lap. His gurgling, in those early hours, with the pain still ringing through my breast, sounded something like a laugh. Only then did I notice my cries had failed to rouse Chris.

Chris has been gone a few days. I have set up a bed in the nursery and sleep there now. I am close enough to tell when Andy needs feeding almost before he does. I hear the change in his breathing that tells me he's about to wake and I am at the cot, ready to lift him out as soon as his eyes open. He is smiling now, proper smiles, not just wind or some random grimace. He beams at me when he wakes with the brightness of a little sun. He warms the surface of me.

Chris leaves messages. He comes round, but I've had the locks changed. I hold Andy up to the double glazing of the bay windows and show him that he's all right, that we're all right, but Chris keeps shouting, so I pull the curtains and he shouts a little more before leaving.

Andy is sleeping now. Look. Have you ever seen such a beautiful baby boy? I can see my mother in him. I wish she were here now. Shhhh. Step back. Listen. Can you hear that? He's waking. I'll feed him first then put the kettle on.

I lean over and say hello. He gurgles at me and I am warm for a minute. My milk draws down, a gushing punch inside my breasts. He strains in my arms, rooting against the fabric of my pyjama top. I stroke his head with one hand and free my breast with the other. He latches on and pulls and a warmth floods my chest as all of me is sucked from inside to out. I stroke his head and he guzzles. At the end of the feed he bites, the pain bright and hot and searing enough to block out everything else, and I do not stop him.

CONNECTING

The laptop arrived early that morning. Maggie signed for it using one of those electronic pads that had somehow replaced pen and paper when she wasn't looking. She frowned at the pixelated approximation of her signature that appeared as she scraped the stylus over the touch-screen.

'It never looks right on these things.'

The courier just smiled and slipped the stylus back in the pad.

Maggie only ever used a computer at work, following an A4 list of instructions written in shorthand and taped to her desk. She often found herself bewildered by the things and hadn't seen the need for owning one before. The laptop was a gift from her son.

'We can keep in touch on the internet,' Malcolm had told her over the phone.

'But I don't know the first thing about computers.'

'You don't need to, Mother.' He only called her that when on the edge of exasperation. 'These days they do all the work for you.'

'If that were true I wouldn't have a job,' she said.

'Mom, I have to go. It'll be with you in a couple of days. Get Brian to help you set it up.'

When Malcolm rang off she sat staring at the phone, the

distance between them always at its greatest after a phone call. His living in London had been bad enough, but he had been in New York for eight months now.

Maggie unboxed the laptop on the kitchen table, revealing a sleek tablet of black and grey which flipped open effortlessly. Her tight-lipped, brow-furrowed reflection stared back from the glossy widescreen. Unfolding the quick-start guide, she barely scanned the set-up instructions before reaching for the phone.

'Brian, hello,' she said when she heard him pick up.

'I saw the courier van. It's arrived has it?'

'Yes. I was just wondering if . . .'

'I take it there's cake.'

'Of course. The kettle's on,' said Maggie, beaming.

'Give me two ticks to tidy up here.'

She liked that about Brian, how tidy he was. He kept himself clean-shaven and dressed well, never mind the fact that he had been retired for, what was it, three years now? He wasn't one of those men who let things slip once his work life ended. She got the mugs ready, lifted the cake dome from over the Victoria sponge and, still smiling, cut a large piece for him.

Brian found Maggie's front door left on the catch.

'You really shouldn't do that,' he said. 'I could have been anyone.'

'Oh, you're not just anyone,' said Maggie, her plump face flushing just a little.

She stirred the teas and passed a steaming mug to Brian.

'No sugar, just how you like it,' she said and busied herself tidying away the used teabags, her floral skirt wafting about her ankles as she worked. 'I still don't know how you can drink it like that.'

'I keep telling you, I'm sweet enough,' Brian smiled.

Maggie handed him the generous slice of Victoria sponge.

'Let's go through,' she said.

Clusters of framed photographs crammed the walls of Maggie's house, the top edges of the frames always free from dust. Brian had spent time exploring the pictures during previous visits. Photography was her late husband's hobby, which explained his absence from most of the photographs. With the exception of a small group of wedding portraits over the sitting room fireplace, the rest of the house documented the upbringing of Maggie's son, Malcolm.

'So, this is it. Nice. These aren't cheap.' Brian nodded towards the laptop.

'Malcolm's done very well for himself,' said Maggie.

He had indeed. Since they became neighbours, Brian had heard a lot about Malcolm from Maggie. She was very proud of her son and had every right to be. Brian often found himself looking at a Malcolm Barr photograph in a broadsheet or lifestyle magazine, and there had been gallery showings in London and New York. Brian knew Maggie hadn't attended either.

'I'll get you sorted out just as soon as I finish this,' he said, taking a large bite out of the slice of sponge cake.

Brian set to work as soon as he drained the last of his tea, booting up the laptop and starting to click through the lengthy set-up process.

'So, you're finally going to join the rest of us in cyberspace. Scared yet?' he called to Maggie who had disappeared into the kitchen with the dirty plates and mugs.

'I'm terrified,' she called back.

The comfortable tone of their raised voices made Brian

smile. He had few friends left and, with the exception of Maggie, none that he saw regularly.

'Don't be. I'll download Skype for you,' he said as Maggie pulled up a chair and leaned in to look at the screen. 'If Malcolm says you need anything else, just let me know.'

Brian continued clicking. He set up a standard user account for Maggie and left it password-free, then created a separate admin account with a password.

'You can use the password to make changes in your account if it asks for it,' he said, 'but probably best to check with me for anything major. Don't want you deleting key files or folders by mistake.'

He looked up to make sure his assumption of her ineptitude hadn't upset Maggie, but she was smiling.

'This is very good of you,' she said.

'Nonsense. Think of it as payment for all those cakes and casseroles you've brought round.'

'Oh, that's just being neighbourly.'

Maggie placed her hand on Brian's. He felt himself tense at the spontaneous contact and she pulled her hand away as if stung.

'Nearly done,' he said.

Keeping his eyes fixed on the screen, Brian brought up the account admin page again, turned the screen towards Maggie, and pointed at a grid of small icons.

'Pick yourself an avatar while I use your loo,' he said. 'Just click one you like.'

Maggie nodded, staring hard at the screen.

In the downstairs toilet Brian grimaced at himself in the mirror.

'Arsehole,' he muttered.

Brian had been aware of Maggie's feelings for him for a while. He liked Maggie and had even once considered, in a particularly isolated moment, that perhaps he could try to pretend with her. He had tried that once before though and knew that the little hurts now saved Maggie the great big one he had inflicted on his ex-wife and daughter. He flushed the toilet and washed his hands.

'I've picked the goldfish,' said Maggie when Brian returned to the dining room.

'Time to get online then. Router in the hall, is it?'

'Router?' Maggie looked baffled. 'There's the Skybox in the living room,' she said.

'Maggie, do you have broadband?'

'We've the TV and phone package. Michael set the contract up for that. He never mentioned any broadband.'

Brian smiled.

'You'll have to get that sorted.'

'So I can't email Malcolm?' Maggie looked crushed.

Brian tapped away on the keyboard for a moment.

'Bingo. My network's showing.' He leapt up from his seat. 'You can use my connection until you get yours sorted. I'll just nip next door and add your laptop to my MAC filter list.'

When Brian got back, he tapped away at the keyboard again, entering a code he had brought with him on a scrap of paper. He said something about MAC addresses and WPA keys. Maggie nodded, but she didn't really understand.

'Just think of it like I'm putting your laptop on my connection's guest list and giving it the invite to get in.'

Maggie nodded again and smiled. That was another thing she liked about Brian, he actually took the trouble to explain things. After Michael died, she had spent a great deal of time struggling to work things like the video recorder or the satellite box. She had struggled for hours setting up the DVD player that Malcolm sent her the Christmas before Brian moved in next door.

As Brian went through how to login to her account on the laptop, Maggie noted down her passwords and instructions on a clean sheet of A4. She listened intently as he showed her how to Google. Brian typed *Malcolm Barr Photography* into the search bar before hitting enter. A list of results appeared on the screen.

'That's Malcolm's website,' he said, clicking the first link.

A minimalist webpage appeared, three words spread across the top of the screen in a large type. *Portfolio. Blog. Contact.* Three photos were arranged in a row across the centre of the screen. A skyscraping view of a Sao Paulo. A baby's foot kicking high into the air above its body, the body in soft focus, the foot sharp and defined, little toes stretching out. The legs of a group of business men marching along a London street, framed from the waist down, still but stepping.

'Does he ever come to visit?' Brian asked as Maggie took the mouse and clicked *Portfolio*.

'He stopped coming home before his father died,' she said.

She clicked through numerous images before stopping on a close-up of an elderly man's face. The stark lighting of the black and white picture artificially darkened his eyes, made each iris a ring of ebony. The man's receded hairline exposed a wrinkled forehead. He stared straight ahead, his lips fixed tightly together.

'That's the only picture Malcolm took of his father,' said Maggie quietly.

Michael was fiercely proud of his son's achievements. Maggie had seen it in her husband's eyes every time Malcolm appeared on TV or sent home a copy of the latest collection of his work. She also saw the disgust Michael couldn't hide when Malcolm came to visit. There were harsh words and Malcolm stopped coming. Then Michael fell ill and Maggie pleaded with both of them to stop the nonsense. Malcolm finally returned home for the funeral, staying just long enough to see the casket in the ground.

Maggie clicked to the blog and scrolled slowly through the most recent posts. She had seen an item on daytime TV about these online diaries; of course Malcolm would have one to document his busy life. Some posts had photographs attached, and they rolled past in time with Maggie's action on the scroll wheel. Eventually she came to rest on a picture of Malcolm with another man. They were sat on a leather sofa, Malcolm leaning in to rest on the stranger. They were holding hands. Maggie smiled.

'They look happy, don't they,' she said quietly.

'I didn't know you knew,' said Brian.

'He's my son,' she said. 'I always knew.'

'My mother never did.'

Maggie turned to look at Brian.

Later, back at home, Brian brooded over a glass of wine. A range of hi-fi equipment sat along one wall of his living room, the stack bookended by two impressive speakers. A wide screen HDTV hung on the wall in front of him. There were no pictures on the walls. Brian sat on a mammoth leather recliner in the centre of the space placed in exactly the optimum viewing and listening position.

The room was silent, the CD he had been listening to long finished. He got up, taking his wine with him, and moved to his PC. Waking the machine, he typed in the URL for his router. Looking at the status page he saw that Maggie was online. He smiled. Good for her. Before coming home, Brian had helped her write the first email she sent to Malcolm. He had waited a while to see if she got a reply, but one hadn't arrived before he left. He hoped it had now.

Brian brought up his own email client and clicked to his contacts. The list was much shorter than it had been when he was married. He deleted his ex-wife's email, along with those of her family and any mutual friends, years ago. Some old work colleagues remained, a few friends of his with whom he had lost touch, but the only other email address in the list for an actual person was his daughter's.

It was an old address. She had probably changed it by now, either when changing ISP or moving to some new internet service. He supposed he could try and send something. If it was returned undeliverable then he could try her prefix at all the major email suffixes. He knocked back his wine and opened a new draft message. He stared at the blank window. His fingers tapped out her name and a comma, then hovered over the keyboard for some minutes before beginning to type.

Stutteringly he composed a first draft before reading back through it, grimacing at each clumsy turn of phrase littering the document. He deleted chunks of the message only to replace them seconds later with a tap of the undo button. He repeated this action, removing and replacing bits of text until, with a groan, he stood and walked away from the keyboard and into the kitchen. He poured himself another glass of wine, took a swig then settled again in front of the screen. With urgent clicks of the mouse, he deleted everything, except:

I am sorry. I miss you. I love you. I am here.
Dad.

Brian checked the email address a final time and typed his daughter's childhood nickname into the subject bar. He dragged the mouse pointer over the send button, held it there.

LOOKING FOR DADDY

'Daddy was poorly and we lost him,' Mummy tells me.

I look for him. I put my arm down the back of the settee like Daddy does when I lose Lego guys, but I don't find him. I look in my wardrobe. He's not there. I look in Mummy and Daddy's. I'm not supposed to go in Mummy and Daddy's room when they don't say, but I go in. Daddy's clothes are thin and quiet. I put on his shoes and jumper and pretend I'm him. I clomp along the landing and do his boomy laugh. I never get it the right loud, but trying is funny.

'Steven, is that you?'

Mummy's coming. I scarper, but Daddy's shoes are big. I tumble. When I get up, Mummy is there.

'I was looking for Daddy,' I say.

She starts crying. I go over and she kneels and cuddles me like she's trying to squeeze me up small. She puts her face against Daddy's jumper. I can see the top of her head. It's weird to see the top of her head. I pat it with my hand. Her crying makes the jumper wet.

I say, 'Don't worry, Mummy, I'll find him,' but it only makes her squeeze me tighter.

STRUTTING AND FRETTING

This is the short and the long of it . . .

'To be, or not to be.' That is the question she asked herself while still only a glint in her mother's womb. To be, she decided and nine months later, burst into the world like an idea newly-formed.

'O wonder!' she thought, her new eyes blinking, sucking up the smiles of her parents. 'How many goodly creatures are there here! How beauteous mankind is! O brave new world. That has such people in't!'

Growing up, she bathed in time and opportunity. Her head brimmed with all she had coming to her. 'The world's mine oyster, which I with sword will open,' she told her career's officer when asked what she wanted to achieve after leaving school.

During University and beyond, she fell for many an unsuitable man. 'Love is blind,' she said when friends reproved her reckless liasons. 'Love looks not with the eyes, but with the mind.'

'Love sought is good, but giv'n unsought is better,' her friends tried to tell her. 'Wisely and slow; they stumble that run fast,' they said.

But each time a lover dumped her by text, she wailed to her friends, 'These words are razors to my wounded heart.' And then each time she cheered, for, as she said, 'To mourn a mischief that is past and gone is the next way to draw new mischief on.'

In her thirties she met a man and lived and loved. She liked to think theirs was a marriage of true minds. The couple did not stray far from their small home and the small life they lived within it. 'For you and I are past our dancing days,' she said.

As her children began callously to pursue their own stories, her husband passed, leaving her to grow old alone. 'When sorrows come, they come not single spies, but in battalions,' she told the warden of the assisted living care home. 'I learnt how sharper than a serpent's tooth it is to have a thankless child,' she said. In the few years that remained she wore her heart upon her sleeve for daws to peck at.

And then was heard no more.

LEAVING
WHAT'S LEFT

I find what's left of my love asleep at the kitchen table, arms folded under a lolling head, face hidden, red hair tumbling over pale skin – a contrast so severe it nearly breaks me to see it. A sudden heaviness fills the bag in my hand, strains my arm. No, not heaviness, that's not quite right. The bag feels as if it's being pulled, like someone small has grabbed the handle, a child perhaps, and is yanking the bag toward the floor. Like gravity but stronger. I look down but there's just the bag and empty space.

'So, you're just going to leave me here?' What's left of my love speaks without raising its head. Its voice is the sound of glass about to crack. It sighs when I don't reply. 'After everything we've been through, you're going to just leave me here.'

It's my turn to sigh now, mine thicker, more of a grunt as I lift the singularity of my packed bag to my shoulder. I step toward the kitchen door and its head flicks up from the cushion of arms. What's left of my love is a girl, it seems, a young woman. Hazel eyes burn out of a pale face which looks like me in places. Hints of myself as a girl peek out from behind the furious curtain of its expression.

'I can't take you with me.' My voice sounds firmer than

it feels in my throat. My heart is a bone in my chest, resilient, rigid, unyielding yet facing the imminent moment of fracture.

'I won't stay here.' It stands with a force that flips the kitchen chair back, crashing it to the tiles.

The dress it wears is one I haven't seen in years, in decades. A mini-skirted floral print that I could never wear now is wrapped around what's left of my love, the flowers a yellowing white that could equally be described as fresh cream or off-milk. On its feet matching leather boots, torn and worn, with long grey socks sprouting out from them, the tops underlining grass stained and grubby knees that, as I notice them, make my breath hurt.

'Be quiet, you'll wake him.'

It smiles at me, teeth sharp, ivory white.

'You're just leaving him too?'

I nod.

'No note?'

I nod.

'Doesn't he at least deserve to be told why.'

I nod, then say, 'He does, but it won't help. Best I just go.'

I move again for the door and it stomps across the kitchen, cuts me off. It taps its right foot in an impatient manner I recognise as my own. Its frame, the look of it, how it holds itself, how it stands, is composed of memories that missed their chance to be made.

It's not quite one thing or the other. It's not wholly like me, like I was back when I was that age, the age this thing, this object, this old emotion is trying to be. It's not like I imagined her to be, either. There is nothing of him in there. Which there should be. Which there would have been. And by him I don't mean my husband who lies in our bed, oblivious to this drama playing out in this early hour in this small dull kitchen in this small dull house. But thinking of my husband of over ten years helps me see what is staring at me. That this thing in front of me, what is left of my love, is impossibly clouded with my husband's features. As if superimposed over the face of what's left of my love. This thing that should look like the other him, the boy, the young man from when I was a girl, a young woman. So distant am I now from the moment that created this love that it has become tainted by everything after. By the compromise and modest happiness that I used to fill the absence inside me.

'Get out of my way.'

I move to go round it. It moves to block me. I move again, again, again and it mirrors me.

'You're not real.' I shove it. Send it sprawling to the floor. Hear its head smack on the tile.

Its cries follow me out of the kitchen, down the hall, out of the house.

'Mother,' it calls after me.

Last week, sitting quietly with the husband I settled for, he on the sofa, me in my chair, he asked me a simple question.

'Any regrets?'

I could feel them all inside me, edges like shoulders rubbing up against each other, jostling to get out. So many that for a moment I said nothing. Had he asked on any other day I might not have hesitated. He wasn't to know. But he asked on the day of the year that brims me with regret more than any other. I have never written that date down. Never needed to. Even back then. Especially back then. I simply carried it in my head, until the accidental child inside me was vacuumed up. That day, more than the day I told the boy, the young man I once loved that it was over, that day was the day I turned my love into something that didn't exist. Something with a half-smile, a hand-me-down dress and grubby knees, that I carried as an outline, as a negative space, while busy making do with the rest of my life. Because, for some reason, way back then, I didn't want a baby. I didn't want a baby with that boy, that young man whose name I can't forget but will never, ever speak. And not wanting that, not wanting that then led me here, to living a life of not wanting.

Last week, sitting quietly with my husband, he on the sofa, me in my chair, I dragged an answer to his simple question from somewhere near my toes and threw it at my tongue.

'No, no regrets,' I said, nearly choking with them.

From there it was just a matter of days passing until I packed a bag and slipped downstairs to find what's left of my love waiting for me in the kitchen.

Outside the daylight-saving sun crawls from behind the trees, head down like a girl, like a young woman desperate to slip into her house, into her room, under her duvet unnoticed, unquestioned. A crunch of leaves accompanies my rapid steps away from the house. A syncopation of smaller feet behind tell me what's left of my love is following. The odd flourish of scattering leaves tells me it is kicking at them with every fifth step or so. Like I used to when things seemed lighter, when there seemed to be time. And like that, my love switches from it to she.

She catches me up as I turn onto Station Road, the red brick buildings huddled along the thin pavement littered with cracked paving slabs.

'Can't I come with you?' She keeps pace with my larger stride, taking two steps for each one of mine. She is careful not to step on the cracks.

'No.'

'Why?'

'I only have enough for one ticket.'

'I don't need a ticket.'

I don't reply.

'Where are you going?'

'Away.'

She pulls a smart phone from the folds of her dress. Of course. She'd have one of those.

'Can I have your number?'

I shake my head.

'Your email?'

'I don't have one.'

I watch her pull that face teenagers pull.

'Who doesn't have email?'

'I don't.'

'Christ, you're not that old.'

We're on the paving slab path that circles the pot-holed tarmac of the station car park. A handful of cars dot the spaces. I stop outside the entrance, sit on the cool plastic seating of the bus shelter. She sits beside me.

'I'll set you one up,' she says.

'I don't need one. No one to email.'

'You could email me.'

I reach out and take her face in my hand, turn her chin toward me, watch her eyes catch mine. Here, in the daylight, away from the house we have both stewed in for years, I finally see something of him in her, something of the boy I loved, that I let go of. I see him and nothing of my husband. I want to tell her this but instead.

'You're not real.'

'Please,' she says, 'how will you manage without me.'

'You were never really with me. You're what could have

been, at best what should have been. Now, I can put you on a bus if you like, send you on your way.'

I slip a two-pound coin into her hand. I check my watch.

'I have to go, my train leaves soon.'

She nods and smiles.

She says, 'Okay.'

And that is when I feel that bone my heart has become, that fierce white structure buried in my chest, that is when I feel it crack and shatter, the whole of it powdering inside me, the waste of me dissolving, drowning in the hammering tumult of my blood.

I close my eyes and hear the pneumatics of brakes beside me. Keep them closed until I hear the release and the growl and throb of the bus as it pulls away. When I open them again the seat beside me is empty and I cross to the station ticket office to see if I have money enough in my purse to get me far enough away.

DID YOU PACK THIS BAG YOURSELF?

Calvin stared into his coffee, certain that everyone in the airport could tell he was a virgin. Raising his head only every now and then to check the departure updates flickering down the screen opposite the café, he did not look at, let alone, God forbid, make eye contact with any of the strangers flowing by. Still, he could feel their eyes upon him, could hear somewhere in the clouds of voices drifting through the terminal that they were all talking about him. He could feel their pity, their disgust.

But not for much longer. He would soon see for himself what all the fuss was about. He had planned his trip meticulously: the flights, the city he would be staying in, the location of the hotel; every part had been carefully selected for the ease with which it might propel him into the arena of the sexually active. Every part except one.

'Calvinsweetheart, I asked if it was time to check-in our bags?'

Calvin pulled his eyes and thoughts away from the board. He stared at Mother as she arched her eyebrow.

'Calvinsweetheart?' She always said it like this, as if it were one word. 'Did you hear what I said?'

'Yes, Mother.'

'Well, is it time?'

Calvin checked his watch.

'We have a little time,' he said. 'Finish your tea and then we'll take the bags over.'

'Didn't I tell you it was worth leaving a few hours early, dear? This way we get to relax before the rush of check-ins and boarding calls. When your father was alive, Godresthim, we were always in a rush, running late. Did I ever tell you about the time we flew to Bermuda . . .'

Calvin stopped listening and watched her mouth moving. Over the years he had grown adept at shutting out her droning. He nodded now and again, but let his thoughts drift back to the trip. If he could just get Mother settled in the hotel, she might well have an early night and he could still get away and explore a bit, begin to put his plan in motion. Forty-two years was quite old enough to still be a virgin. For goodness' sake, there were Hollywood movies lampooning the sad state of his personal life. It was time to do something about it.

Calvin originally booked the trip for one, but was forced to plump for another ticket when Mother, during one of her searches of his room while he was out at work, found where he had hidden his.

'There must be no secrets between us,' she had said. 'Don't you want your old mum to have a holiday too?'

He had shook his head just as he did when a child.

'That's settled then. I mean, who wants to go on holiday on their own?'

Uncomfortable on the hard plastic of the airport café chair, Calvin cringed at the memory of his spinelessness. He watched Mother place her cup and saucer onto the tray.

'Are you okay, Calvinsweetheart? You don't look well.'

Calvin shrugged. 'I'm fine,' he said and shook his head to clear it a little. 'We should go check-in the bags.'

'As you like, dear,' Mother said.

Calvin stood and took her tweed travel jacket from the back of her chair, waited as she checked her purse, stood and smoothed down her skirt.

'Thank you, dear,' she said as he helped her into the jacket. 'Such a polite boy.'

She stretched up to kiss his cheek. Calvin felt his teeth grit as she did so.

'You're welcome, Mother,' he said.

In the check-in queue, Calvin waited while Mother rummaged through her purse.

'There we are,' she said and handed Calvin the tickets and passports. 'Now don't go losing them. I want them straight back.'

Calvin nodded and wheeled their luggage forward a few inches with the movement of the queue. He gripped his hand luggage: a laptop bag strapped across his chest in case anyone should try to snatch it. His laptop, a necessity in his line of work, was his only private space. Mother's dislike of modern digital devices meant Calvin had somewhere to retreat where she couldn't follow. Nor could she argue over the time he spent on it in his room. He had to work, he told her when she tried.

The laptop had made the trip possible. The planning, the booking of tickets. Most importantly, the abundance of social networks available through it had helped him find Cilla. Calvin could barely believe that she was waiting for him, only a short flight standing between them and meeting in the flesh.

'Passports, please.'

Calvin looked about him. He was at the head of the queue.

'Give the nice lady the passports, Calvinsweetheart,' Mother said, nudging him in the ribs.

Calvin handed over the passports, a frail smile playing over his lips. He hefted his suitcase onto the conveyer.

'Did you pack this bag yourself?'

Calvin nodded. The check-in girl stared at him.

'Yes, I did,' he added, nodding harder.

'And, your wife?'

'Oh she's, she's, oh she's . . .' Calvin felt something knot inside him as his mother beamed at the check-in girl. She enjoyed these mistakes as much as they sickened him.

'Oh, my dear girl, I'm his mother.'

The check-in girl examined the passports. 'I beg your pardon,' she said, 'my mistake.'

The further Calvin moved into middle-age, the more people assumed the pair were man and wife. Even Calvin had to admit his mother did not look her age, while he seemed so much older than his. It was as if time were addressing the imbalance of their years, bridging the gap by taking from her to give to him.

'No problem.' Calvin felt his stomach tighten as the check-in girl attached labels to the suitcases.

'Please be sure your hand-luggage fits the guide frames provided,' the check-in girl said, handing back the passports.

Calvin nodded, watching the suitcases move along the conveyor and disappear behind the fringes of plastic strip. He half-expected alarms to go off and security to abseil down on ropes from the ceiling. Nothing happened.

'If you could move along, sir,' the check-in girl said.

Calvin looked round, mouthed a weak apology to those

behind him, handed the passports and tickets back to his mother, then wheeled the empty trolley out of the queue.

Wheeling the trolley back to the stand, the tightness washed through him again. A repeat of the check-in girl's mistake played over in his head. He thought again of his luggage making its way through the bowels of the airport, passing through X-rays and scanners, being sniffed by dogs trained to find contraband, and the tightness grew.

Calvin shoved the trolley into the rank, the smack of metal on metal swallowed in the noise of the airport. His guts squeezed harder.

'I have to go,' he blurted to Mother and started to run for the gents near the entrance to Departures.

'Is everything all right, Calvinsweetheart?' Mother called after him, but he did not look back.

He slammed the men's room door open and dived into the nearest cubicle, just managing to sit, his trousers and pants round his ankles, before a hot stream of shit splattered into the toilet bowl. His backside bubbled, squirting only dribs and drabs for a second before something inside him flipped. He groaned as his innards slopped into the water beneath him.

Calvin sucked a deep breath through his mouth and placed his palms on the cubicle walls to steady himself. The flow slowed again to a dribble and stayed there. He sat and waited for it to stop. The whole misunderstanding with the check-in girl had been the final straw, but what was really bothering him was what was inside his luggage. He wished he hadn't packed the bloody thing, but there was nothing to be done now his suitcase was on its way to the plane. He could ditch what he had in his hand luggage, but that wouldn't matter if they found the rest of it tucked in amongst his socks and in the pockets of his wash-bag. At least he had had the sense to dismantle it into its components before packing it, in the hope that it would seem less conspicuous to anyone looking at his baggage.

He bought the pump from a website specialising in those sort of things and had to cancel his credit card after unusual payments began appearing on his statements. His embarrassment stopped him from filing a report with the credit card company over the fraudulent use of his card, or complaining to the website when the item failed to arrive. About three months later, when he had just started to forget the whole thing, a parcel wrapped in brown paper appeared at his place of work. He smuggled it home.

The men in the videos he downloaded from the internet when Mother was sleeping had driven him to such measures. They all seemed so big. This particular pump, if you believed the testimonials of the spam emails, was capable of increasing male member size by up to fifty percent. The cost of the additional charges to his credit card were a small price to pay if it worked. He could hardly hope to satisfy a woman like Cilla with his pathetic, natural girth.

His bowels having settled, Calvin remained seated and flushed the toilet, allowing the cold water to splash him in the hope it might make cleaning himself a little easier. As he stood to begin wiping himself he heard the door to the gents open.

'Calvinsweetheart, are you okay in there?'

Calvin winced.

'I'm fine, Mother, wait outside.'

'They'll be calling our flight soon.'

'I'll be right there, Mother, please. Wait for me outside.'

He heard her footsteps moving towards his cubicle.

'It smells like someone has a tummy upset.'

From the sound of her voice she was just the other side of his cubicle door.

'Mother, please!'

'Don't you "Mother please" me, you know how you get with your irritable bowel. Now open this door and let me help you.'

Calvin wiped his arse one final time, before flushing the toilet and hoisting his trousers up.

'See, I'm fine,' he said, opening the cubicle and marching to the sinks.

'Be sure and wash your hands properly.'

Calvin watched his mother leave the gents in the mirror over the sinks, then washed his hands and splashed cold water on his face. He stepped back and looked himself up and down. A weak smile flashed across his face, but vanished quickly as a wave of self-pity threatened to send him running back to the toilet.

He sucked in a deep breath, adjusted the collar of his shirt, shook his head and scurried out.

Mother slipped her hand onto the inside of his elbow as he exited. The pair walked across the departure lobby, heading for the security check. They joined the queue and began to snake round in silence along with the others.

'Calvinsweetheart, have I done something to upset you?' Mother reached up and pushed his fringe across his face, sorting out the parting in his hair. He felt himself bristle.

'No, Mother.'

They were nearing the head of the queue and Calvin removed his belt and jacket ready to place in the grey plastic trays.

'Good, now where would you like to go tonight?'

Calvin stood silent for a moment.

'I have plans,' he said, quietly, straining to keep his voice level.

Mother looked up at him, her eyebrow once again arched. Calvin watched her raise her hands, putting one either side of his face. He felt the points of her long red nails press the skin of his cheeks.

'Calvinsweetheart,' she said, pulling his face down toward hers, 'you can't possibly leave me alone our first night in a strange city.'

Calvin felt her grip tighten a fraction as she said this. He mumbled an answer.

'What's that, dear?'

'I have a date.'

Calvin flinched as he said this, squinting to take in Mother's response.

'A date? A date with whom? You don't know anybody? You certainly don't know anybody in Barcelona.'

Calvin squirmed in her grip, looking left and right. The people in front and behind in the queue stared nervously at the pair and stepped back. At the security terminals ahead, Calvin saw a burly female security guard take a step towards them.

'Mother, you're causing a scene.'

'No, Calvin, I am reacting to your inconsiderate behaviour which is wholly unbecoming of a good son,' said Mother, the shrillness of her voice increasing with the steady metronome of each syllable. 'How you can think of seeing some trollop, when – '

'Her name is Cilla. I met her on the internet.'

Calvin looked Mother in the eye and spoke slowly. Her mouth flapped open and closed for a moment and Calvin exhaled heavily.

'I knew it. The hours you spend on that vile machine

had to be more than just work.' Mother released Calvin's face and made a grab for the laptop bag. 'How can you think of meeting some filthy whore from the internet.'

They had reached the front of the queue and Calvin stepped forward, placing his jacket, wallet, keys and belt in one of the trays and his laptop bag directly on the conveyor behind it, careful to keep himself between his mother and the conveyor.

'My goodness Calvin, can't you see you're being groomed? Cilla won't be her real name.'

Mother made to step around him, but Calvin shuffled with her, kept himself between her and the conveyor.

'I know it's not her real name. She told me her real name. She's told me everything about herself.'

'Calvinsweetheart, how could you?' There was no self-pity or vulnerability in Mother's voice as she said this, just animal snarling.

Calvin felt his stomach twist further, but stood still, refusing his mother everything, even fear.

'I knew you wouldn't understand Mother, you always . . .'

Calvin stopped himself, aware his voice was rising to a shout, aware people were staring.

'Is everything okay, sir? Madam?'

The female security officer eyed Calvin and his mother. Calvin felt the knot in his stomach tighten again as Mother glared back at the guard.

'Yes, thank you. Simply a private matter between a mother and her son.'

Calvin felt his face fill with heat.

'Shoes, please, sir.'

The security officer pointed at Calvin's feet. He bent, unlaced his shoes and placed them on the conveyor. He stepped forward to meet the woman's male colleague, a tall, dark-skinned man with a severe crew cut. Calvin realised, as the man's large hands patted him down, that this was his first physical contact with a human being who wasn't his mother in years. Too many years. He felt his stomach tighten again and groaned as the security guard checked his legs.

'Are you all right, sir?' The security guard stopped, crouched down with his hands either side of Calvin's left leg. He looked up at Calvin and waited for an answer.

'Fine, I'm fine,' managed Calvin.

The frisking finished, Calvin stepped through the metal detector. The barrier remained silent. He stood on the other side of the detector and looked back at his mother as the female security officer performed her physical check. Calvin felt the urge to run taunting him, stronger than ever, because here, surrounded by security barriers and trained security personnel, he was even more trapped than usual.

He pushed the feeling down as his laptop bag trundled up the conveyor, the knot inside him tightening with every shove. Calvin concentrated on putting his belt back on.

'Is this bag yours, sir?'

Another female security officer, this one from amongst the staff behind the conveyor's X-ray scan, held Calvin's laptop bag in the air before him.

Calvin stared at the bag and a feeling of falling rushed through him.

'Yes, it is.'

'Did you pack this bag yourself?'

Calvin nodded.

'Could you speak up, sir?' the official said.

'Yes, I packed the bag myself.'

'According to the X-ray there appears to be a suspicious item inside. Could you please follow me?'

Calvin followed the official around to the rear of the security station where the conveyor ended and a table top sat between Calvin and the security officer.

'Calvinsweetheart? Is everything okay?'

Calvin looked over to where Mother was slipping on her shoes.

'Fine, Mother, they just want to check my bag.'

'Could you tell me if there is anything requiring declaration in this piece of luggage?' The security officer said this loudly. Calvin understood the rise in volume was intended as a full stop to his conversation with Mother.

'No. Just a laptop and few personal items.'

The security officer placed the laptop bag onto the tabletop between them and slowly unzipped the main compartment. Calvin watched the woman's thick masculine fingers pull the zip around the case, enjoying their contrast with the deep pink polish on her nails. The tightness in his stomach moved further down, becoming something like arousal. She flipped the lid and Calvin gasped involuntarily. He felt sweat forming on his brow.

'Sir, are you okay?'

'Fine, I'm fine,' Calvin said, dabbing at his forehead with his handkerchief.

He smiled weakly at her as she stared at him. She tapped a finger on the laptop case and he was glad to have an excuse to look away.

'There is nothing here that you want to explain.'

Calvin stared at the case. He knew what she was getting at. It was right there, nestled in the pocket of the bag designed for a computer mouse. He thought he had been so clever.

'Sir?'

Calvin felt himself freeze, ice sweeping down his spine, locking him in place.

The security officer reached out her manicured hand and plucked the item from the pocket. A sickening exhilaration reached into Calvin's limbs as he watched her hold the item up between them.

It was black and made of rubber and looked something like a hand grenade. A valve stuck out from the top, a connection for some sort of device. The security guard gave it a slight squeeze, a squeak of air escaping the top.

'Calvinsweetheart, what's happening?'

Calvin looked across to where a male security officer was attempting to shepherd her along.

'Young man, I will move along as soon as you return my son.'

Her voice was becoming shrill.

'Sir?'

Calvin turned back to the female security officer.

'Could you explain exactly what this is?' she asked, still holding the hand grenade-shaped piece of rubber. 'Sir?'

Calvin felt his voice catch in his throat, coughed to clear it and tried again. 'It's part of a pump,' he said in a whisper.

'I beg your pardon?'

The security officer's eyes tightened and she took a step forward.

'Please speak up, sir.'

Calvin tried to raise his voice.

'It's part of a penis pump,' he said again, his eyes moving nervously to where his Mother was standing, still fighting security's attempts to move her on.

'I said, speak up, sir.' The female security guard waved a

hand as she said this and Calvin watched as two more security officers, men, moved around the station toward him.

Calvin laughed nervously and tried again.

'It's a pump,' he mumbled to the woman holding the black rubber squeezer.

He had just time to watch her eyes widen before the two men were on him, pushing him to the floor.

'It's just a pump,' he tried to say, but somewhere between his accent and the anxious speed of his words they were hearing something else.

Calvin felt a knee pushing into his spine and squealed. One of the officers pushed his face hard to the floor and Calvin could just see Mother, held in place by another two security officers.

'Calvinsweetheart!' she bellowed. Then to the men holding her, 'You leave my boy alone. Leave him be.'

'Potential bomb alert. Suspect is restrained and device appears to be dismantled at present,' Calvin heard the female officer say into her radio.

'Don't fuckin' move.'

This second voice, thick and male and close to Calvin's ear, came from one of the men restraining him. Calvin thought about prison. He wondered if Cilla would write to him. The floor cold against his cheek, Calvin watched Mother's pudgy ankled foot stomp in time with her squeals of protest, and he smiled.

WHAT PRECISE
MOMENT

Georgina Samson woke from troubled dreams to find herself transformed into a vending machine. She stood in the kitchen, beside the fridge, a convenient spot that anyone entering or leaving would have to pass. Unable to cry out, she could do nothing but wait for her family to appear and unravel exactly what it was that had happened to her.

Milton, her youngest, was the first to enter the kitchen that morning.

'Beckfast,' the three-year-old said, slurring the word sleepily.

He spoke directly into a flat, round microphone set into her casing that felt, to Georgina Samson's ruffled mind, not so unlike an ear. Deep inside her workings she felt something mechanical shift and rotate and tip, followed by the sound of flakes hitting ceramic and a chill feeling, almost like wetting oneself, flooded through the lower regions of her chassis.

She watched Milton pull open a flap in her front and remove a bowl of cereal.

'Tanks, Mam,' he said before taking himself off to the table.

Georgina watched him seat himself and begin to eat, more than a little proud of how he managed it all with a minimum of fuss and mess.

Someone thumping her smooth glass front wrenched her back to her strange predicament.

'I said, toast.' Violet, her eldest whacked her again. 'C'mon mother, Paul's picking me up in a minute.'

Georgina's insides grew hot and fiery and she thought she might be about to explode, but it was simply the toast popping inside her. Violet yanked the somehow-buttered slices from Georgina's hatch and raced out the back door to the yard.

'I'm late!' she yelled back at her mother.

Last down was Michael, stuffing papers into his brief-case.

'Just coffee for me, dear.'

Heat filled her again, this time fluid and drenching, flushing through her with cystitic urgency. A creamy cool-ness followed. Finally she spat something granulated into the mix.

Michael lifted the flap and gently removed the paper cup. He planted a quick kiss on her hardened exterior, grabbed his keys from her top, where he must have left them, and headed out.

Her inner workings still for the first time that morning, Georgina Samson watched Milton finish his breakfast, and wondered when it was exactly, what precise moment of her marriage, her motherhood, it was that she turned into this.

YOU MIGHT STILL

Driving the motorway, a needle's flicker over fifty in the middle lane, vehicles flurry by to the left and right, and I scan their windows for a glimpse of you. M6, M5, M42, M40, A34, M40, M42, M5, M6. I make a loop of the route you used to take. The route you might still.

A squeeze of accelerator or tap of the brake pushes or pulls me alongside cars I wish to double-take. Cars you might drive. A new model Fiesta in blue. An original Beetle, green with a sunflower decal blooming over the rear left wheel arch. A Mini just like the one you used to drive back then, before we moved in together, before you moved out.

You drove this route to see me, I drove it to see you. Sometimes we drove in convoy, me in my worse-for-wear Escort, taking two cars up to mine or down to yours, one of us needing to head off somewhere else at some point for work. Coffee and a pale pastie at Warwick services. Pulling faces at each other in the rear-view mirror of whoever was in front.

I check behind me but you are not there. A sign next to the hard shoulder reads *Tiredness can kill*. I pull off at the next exit and follow the signs to the petrol station. Thirty litres, a packet of crisps and a Coke. I put the car in a parking space and stretch my legs while I eat and drink, watching the carriageways, hoping I don't miss you.

Back in the car I do the usual and wait for you to pass me. The caffeine from the Coke has me alert and watchful. I put on the CD I burnt for you, the one I plan to play when I find you, to make sure the songs are just right. As the music plays, the odd tear blurs my vision and I have to wipe them away fast so as not to miss a glimpse.

Not for the first time I imagine you driving the opposite carriageway, heading in the other direction, destined to pass me and I'd never know because I'm the wrong side of the central reservation. In my head I stare down at the motorway, the six lanes of traffic flashing this way and that, and I see us pass, just metres away from each other, never knowing.

At the next exit I turn off and find myself on a roundabout. I turn a complete circuit, passing the two feed-on lanes, the two feed-off lanes of the motorway. I turn another circuit and imagine you on your way south, heading down the country like you used to when we were together, like you might still. I see the feed-off lane for the south-bound traffic and turn my steering wheel hard to get the car onto it. Someone hammers their horn behind me and I hear a screech of brakes, but I am across and heading up the off-ramp. I try to imagine the look on your face when you see me heading north on the southbound carriageway to meet you.

SILHOUETTE
OF A LADY

He found her the first night in his new flat, hidden behind a monolithic oak wardrobe abandoned by the previous tenant. Unable to sleep, intimidated by its looming bulk, he decided to shift it to the hall, tip it in the morning. Shuffling the shabby, battered thing across the carpet, he revealed the life-size silhouette painted on the Oxford Blue wall behind, the white of her body stark as a retinal after-image. The style of her hair, the cut of her clothes, the shape of her shoes, all could be correlated from the detailed outline. Inside, written in precise black ink swirls, a flurry of adjectives, phrases, sentences, coiled about each other, all in the same hand, running in all directions, some at right angles, others upside down, as if whoever wrote them had sat and stood in a myriad of positions to set them down.

He placed a lamp upon the floor at the end of his bed and sat beside it, his face and the bulb pointed up at the silhouette. He read every word.

'You need to forget her,' his best friend said in the pub the next night.

But he wasn't thinking about his ex at all. His mind was full of the silhouette. If he closed his eyes he could see her.

He had avoided unpacking by reading and re-reading the words inside her. That afternoon, lying on his back, feet on his pillow, head dangling upside down from the end of the bed, he had committed them to memory.

A number of young women were dotted about the pub, some with boyfriends, some in groups. In his head, he held them up against the silhouette and found them, one after another after another, wanting. But he knew in his gut she was out there somewhere.

'I can't,' he said to his best friend. It was easier than explaining and, anyway, he found that he did not wish to share her.

Later that week, his ex called round. She looked great. He could see that. She perched on his second-hand sofa, surrounded by his still-unpacked boxes, and called through to where he was making coffee in the kitchen.

'I think we're making a mistake,' she said.

He pretended not to hear and she repeated the statement as he carried in the drinks. He sat in the chair opposite. Over her shoulder he could see through to his bedroom.

'We're definitely making a mistake,' she said.

As she continued, he tried his best to concentrate on what she was trying to tell him. He had, after all, until very recently, loved her very much. But the shape on the wall kept catching his eye, beckoning him back to the bedroom.

SOILED

It's still dark out when I start reversing the van and see Len crunching down the drive towards me in his slippers and dressing gown, head bowed like he's walking in the rain. I stop and wind down the window.

'Morning, Len.'

He scuffs past, mumbling a blur of words and making a beeline for the front door. I yank the handbrake and hop out to cut him off before he wakes Fi and the kids.

'All right there, mate, what's got you out of bed so early?'

Len triggers the front porch motion sensor. He blinks, frozen in the dazzle of the security light.

'You okay there, mate?'

His body shivers, his white whiskered jaw chattering. He arches the twig thin fingers of both hands into the air in front of him as if holding something, shaking something.

'Fuckin' toilet,' he says.

His hands squeeze into fists, his face tightens around bared, yellowing teeth.

'Fuckin' shittin' fuckin' toilet,' he says, his voice straining to escape his wheezing chest.

I put my hand on his shoulder. He smells of stale piss and bad drains.

'Let me help you, Len,' I say and watch as the spell lifts and he finally sees me.

'Jake?' he says.

'Jake,' I say.

He smiles at me. Then clouds return to his eyes.

'Fuckin' toilet,' he says.

I put my arm around his shoulders and we start back up the drive. Reckon I can drop him back, as it's only down the road, and head off from there.

'Let's get you home and you can tell me all about it on the way,' I say, helping him up into the passenger seat of the van.

In the time it takes to walk round to the driver's seat, the smell from Len has filled the cab. I leave my window down, put the van in gear and reverse out.

Len mutters and rocks in the passenger seat. His eyes peer out through the windscreen, flicking this way and that, searching for something and not finding it. I turn right and think about switching on the radio, but Len's house is only halfway up the next street. Len's face brightens a little as he sees his house. The overgrown lawn and peeling paint on the window frames look out of place in the otherwise tidy row. The front door swings wide open, anyone could walk in.

'Fuckin' bastard toilet,' Len says as I help him out the van. His body feels papery; the fabric of his housecoat has more substance.

'What's the problem with the toilet? I've got the tools in the van. I could have a look for you.'

Len stops at the door to the house.

'Jake,' he says, the fog lifting. 'I'm sorry.'

Not really sure what he is sorry for, I check my watch. Should be okay. As long as it isn't too big a job, I shouldn't be too late.

The smell of the house swamps me as I follow Len in.

Sweat, shit and something like rotten meat. The hall is dark, the curtains pulled closed at the top of the stairs. Len starts the slow climb up. I flick the landing light on and follow.

'So, what's the problem with the toilet, Len?'

He mumbles something I can't hear.

'Sorry mate, what was that?'

He stops on the stairs in front of me and turns his head slow, like a turtle. 'The bloody thing's blocked.'

'Not a problem, mate, I can sort that.'

He stares at me blankly then turns and continues up.

At the top of the stairs he stops and stands outside the closed bathroom door, hanging his head. I put my toolbox down on the landing carpet and tug the curtains open. The dawn sun spills through the glass, dust showering down through the beam. Len doesn't look up or tell me to go in.

I nudge the bathroom door open and raise a hand to catch my gag. The floor of the bathroom is swimming in foul water. Clumps of loo paper, stained with browns and yellow, form little islands in the slop.

Tears slip down Len's face, collecting in his whiskers before dripping onto the collar of his pyjamas. I make my voice jolly and steer him back to the stairs.

'Right, Len mate, let's get you downstairs and make a cuppa, then I'll see about sorting the loo.'

The kitchen, a battlefield of dirty pots, smells almost as bad as the bathroom. I sit Len at the table, raise the blind to let some light in, and set about finding the kettle. Looking at the state of things I decide not to make myself a drink. While the kettle boils, Len rocks and mumbles in his seat. In the gap of his housecoat I see food stains on his pyjamas.

Time was, Len would always be well turned out. 'Can't abide scruffiness,' he told me once, years back now, when

I was seeing his Tracy. Len complained about the 'scruffy apeths' on the telly. He'd sit in his chair and grumble from behind the local headlines as Tracy and I revised our exams, Dexy's jigging to 'C'mon Eileen' on the TV. 'Look smart,' he told me. I made sure I turned up in a decent shirt after that.

I pass Len his tea in the cleanest mug I can find, but a skin of scum still floats on the top. Is it really less than two years since his Joan died? Looking at the state of the house, of Len, it seems like such a short time for things to get so bad.

'Does Tracy not come round to see you?'

Len looks up, eyes eager and hopeful.

'Is Tracy coming?' He puts his cup down on the table and the shaking starts again. His head nods up and down. 'Is Tracy coming?'

'Maybe later,' I say. 'Why don't you tell me about the toilet?'

Len's face brims with anger and he starts again with the 'Fuckin' toilet.'

'Hold on, Len,' I say and crouch down to look him in the eye, 'tell me what happened.'

'It's that doctor,' he says and slams a fist onto the table. The jolt slops the tea into a puddle around his mug. His eyes are clear now, focused. 'Sometimes I can't shit. Some-times I can't stop. He's done tests. Stuck stuff up my arse. That barium bollocks. The useless bastard still isn't sure what's what. He told me to keep a diary.'

'A diary?'

Len stares, as if seeing me in the room for the first time.

'Of my bowel movements.'

We stare at each other for a minute. I don't know who starts first but we both laugh at this.

'A diary of my shit. Bloody mental, right?' Len says. 'And they say I'm going funny in the head.'

Len stops laughing, picks up his dripping mug of tea. He takes a sip and spits it out across the table.

'You forgot the bloody sugar,' he says, pointing at the bowl on the cluttered worktop.

I pass him the bowl and he spoons in seven sugars. He sips the tea again, adds three more and seems satisfied.

'You sit there, drink your tea and I'll sort out upstairs,' I say.

Len nods and begins to slurp his tea as I head off to the van to grab my phone from the glove compartment and my toolbox from the back. On my way back up the stairs I press call on my work number and tell them I'm going to be late. 'Family emergency,' I say, though Len isn't. Still, I can't leave him like this.

A dark stain arches into the landing carpet where it meets the bathroom lino, the water soaking over the gripper separating the two. I step into the bathroom and the water laps lightly around the soles of my work boots. The bathroom suite is so grime-ridden it's hard to tell the original colour. A bucket sits inside the shower stall. I don't need to look to know what Len's been using it for.

Dried yellow stains splatter the toilet seat, while in the bowl, just visible through the pool of rank water threatening to flood the lip, streaks of shit cling to the sides. The shades of yellow and brown remind me of Len's teeth. I open the window wide, balance my toolbox across a corner of the bath and flip the lid.

Gloves on, I scoop the excess water from the toilet with a manky cup from the sink, slopping it into the shower bucket. The water dissolves some of the filth inside, releasing more of the foul smell. I plunge the toilet a few times, waiting to feel something move in the vacuum, but there's nothing, so I uncoil the flexible cleaning tool and insert it into the U-bend. I try to rotate it, but something stops the tool from turning fully in the pipe. I stab it down and feel the blockage shift slightly. I shove it again and watch the water level in the bowl fall. I flush the loo a couple of times, then empty the bucket into the bowl and flush again. Happy things are moving in the right direction, I head back downstairs.

Len is still sat at the kitchen table.

'That's all fixed for you, just need to check the drain,' I say. 'That room's going to need a bloody good clean, mind.'

Len looks up as if seeing me for the first time.

'Is Tracy with you?' he says, then turns his head fast about, searching.

'No, Len, she's not.'

'Where's Tracy?' he says, rocking again, his arms wrapped around himself.

I crouch so he can meet my eyes. 'I'll call her for you.'

I find the address book, smothered in dust, by the phone in the hall and put Tracy's number in my mobile before going back outside to fetch the drain tool from the van.

'You've reached Tracy, leave a message,' the phone says.

'Tracy, it's Jake. You need to come see your dad.' From inside the house I hear Len swearing loudly about the toilet. 'Christ, Tracy how long has it been since you've seen him? Have you seen the state of him? The state of the house? Call me when you get this, or better still, get your-self round here and help the poor bugger.'

I snap the phone shut, stuff it in my pocket and set about lifting the drain cover round the side of the house. In the weak stream of effluent lies a small black book. I lift it out with a gloved hand and flick through pages soaked yellow and brown. In the centre, near the spine, a circle of pure white paper cores the book where the filthy water hasn't reached. The last entry is three days ago. The pages are scrawled with brief notes. I make out words like *lots of straining today* and *nothing* and *some blood and pain* in clear black ink on the white semicircle of each page. On the stained parts of the pages the ink has smudged into a thick black unreadable trails.

'What the bloody hell are you doing?'

Something smacks me hard in the back of the head, knocking me off balance. I sprawl forward, my foot catching on the manhole lip and I roll to the side to stop my left leg dropping into the drain hole. Looking up from where I lie on my back I see Len stood over me, fists clenched. He is wearing just his pyjamas now. Food stains paint the front of them, sauces dried to the colour of blood. The knees of the trousers are mud stained and dark browns and yellows streak down from the gusset.

'You sniffing round my Tracy again? I warned you what'd happen if I caught you round here.'

I find my feet and stand, rubbing the back of my head. Len still packs a punch. His eyes tell me he is back over twenty years to when Tracy and I were doing A levels, back to when he thought what happened was my fault.

'You stay away from my girl.' Len shakes as much from the cold of the early morning as the anger he is reliving.

'Len, I – ,' I start to say, but he shuffles a few hurried steps toward me and swings again and, like years ago, I can't explain to him that Tracy was the one who fucked everything up. I step back and he flails at the air and tries again. I retreat until my back is at the fence.

'I'm not going to fight you, Len,' I say, 'this was a long

time ago. Somewhere in there you know I wasn't to blame. Tracy told you the truth, years ago. You told me that.'

Len swings again and I dodge the fist easily. The next punch I catch and pull him toward me as gently as I can with him struggling. I still have the diary. He strains to free himself, but simply doesn't have the strength to get away.

'Len, it's okay. I stayed away like you told me.'

His eyes rage just like they did years ago. I could try to fill him in on the time since then – Tracy telling him the truth, his apology to me, bad feeling fading over beers down the Feathers when we bumped into each other at the end of a working week – but he won't hear me.

I wave the diary under his nose.

'You stuffed this down the toilet and blocked the bloody system,' I say.

Len's eyes cloud and his body goes limp. I chuck the diary down next to the drain and help him over to the garden bench.

'Fuckin' toilet,' he says.

'Fuckin' toilet,' I say.

I fetch a coat for him from the house and we sit outside in the fresh air for a bit, the day starting without us.

'Is Tracy coming?' he says.

'Soon, Tracy's coming soon,' I say.

AN UNIMAGINED
WOMAN

Upon the death of her mother, Ruth Butterfield's husband waited only a superficially respectable month or so before demanding a divorce.

'I'm in love with Tessa,' he told her as they lay, post-coital in their marital bed, the sheets still warm and wet. Of course, Ruth thought, the secretary.

'And the sex?' she asked, wanting him to explain why he had chosen to bed her as a prologue to his news.

'Just fantastic,' he said and rolled over.

Ruth had, up until this moment, considered their marriage tolerable in most areas. They did not often clash, though this was more due to her willingness to please him than any reciprocation on his part. From the start, Ruth's married life had been a road traversing first inclines, then foothills and finally mountains of accommodations made to satisfy her husband's desires. Whatever bright liquid sparkle her dark eyes carried as a young woman had long since expired, leaving behind, while not quite a sunken disappointment, at least a level sustainable discontent of which, if anyone had thought to ask her, Ruth herself would have been unaware.

The imbalance of the relationship found outward

expression in the couple's physical appearance. Her tall, solid figure approached a voluptuousness that her quiet nature led her to obscure with a hunch of her shoulders, a bow of her head, as she attempted, like so many tall women married to short, round, domineering men, to shrink herself down. For his part Paul Butterfield compensated for his lack of height by employing elevator shoes, his plump features framed in a salt and pepper beard and inflated with arrogance and self-satisfaction, as if sheer bombast of personality might make him appear taller. A butcher by trade, he spoke in broad sharp sentences, directing them to his wife much as he would the tools of his trade to a side of beef.

Truth be told, theirs was an archaic marriage by modern standards, his thoughts focused always on his work, hers on the crafting of the perfect home. He owned and ran a string of shops across the county, and the Herculean task of keeping his empire afloat in the challenging economic climate in which they found themselves in their middle age took much of his time and all of his concentration. Even in those hours when his physical body occupied the marital home, he could not truly be described as present, so Ruth filled her husband's absence, both physical and emotional, with home improvement magazines and television programmes, furnishing the house with other people's ideas of what an ideal home should be, all the while her husband taking no notice of her efforts.

Had she been more readily inclined to examine her feelings she might have considered her husband's fixation on matters of business, matters of meat, wholly vulgar. As it was, she avoided thinking of her husband's business much at all. She had certainly never allowed herself to regard his profession as any objection to making him a husband. Indeed, she developed the habit of not thinking about his work during their engagement and merely continued that habit into the steadily growing years of their married life. She came not to notice the meaty smell he carried home and, like a person fearful of something lurking in the dark, refused to reflect on what she had traded herself for, and so had no idea of her marriage's worth, rare or common, gold, silver or lead, until this moment.

Awake and for the first time truly considering her situation, Ruth arrived at the following conclusion: in the natural progression that attends most if not all marriages under the practical conditions which society crafts for its fruition, clearly whatever love might have existed between them had not survived except in the irregular shape of a strained and sober partnership. Obviously her husband was still a man with desires beyond that of companionship, which in turn had led to his hitching himself to a younger, more receptive woman. Ruth understood all of this, lying in the dark beside his thickly snoring bulk, but whether because of the distance between them, which over the years had yawned from a crack to a chasm in unrelenting increments, or some manifestation of shock, she felt very little.

Following his revelation, Paul Butterfield did not move out. Nor did he ask Ruth to leave, seeming happy to have her continue residence in a purely custodial role. He chose instead to immediately install his new lover, Tessa, in the marital home. Ruth moved into the guest bedroom without argument. She spent her days alone in the house much as she always had, with Paul returning late from work much as he always had, and she would have noticed little difference in their lives before and after his revelation had it not been for the presence of Tessa.

The evening she arrived, nothing was said about the strangeness of it all. Paul poured himself and Tessa a large drink from the cabinet while Ruth, her mother's passing having rekindled her interest in genealogy, studied her family tree in silence. *Eastenders* blaring unwatched from the TV, the adulterous pair fumbled drunkenly on the sofa as if Ruth were not sat in her armchair leafing through pages of notes and old letters arranged on a tray upon her lap.

'Oh, Paul, no, stop it,' squawked Tessa.

Ruth looked up to see her husband, forehead red and sweaty, damp patches darkening the pale blue of his shirt, half-lying on the stick-thin Tessa, a hand stuffed up her top. Tessa was older than Ruth had expected, her baby-doll tee and mini-skirt only just avoiding the mutton-dressed-as-lamb-effect that a few more years would bring.

'Make me.' The frantic wriggling of Paul's hand under the hot-pink fabric of the T-shirt looked to Ruth as if a small animal were flailing to get out.

'You know I can.' Tessa countered with a grab at his crotch, her fingers spread into a tightly squeezing claw.

'Ohh, harder,' grinned Paul, placing his own meaty hand over Tessa's.

Ruth gasped at this and the pair turned on her.

'What?' Paul leered at Ruth as he spoke. 'She's only doing what you could have done years ago if you hadn't been such a prude.'

'Ignore her, Paul. Let's go upstairs.'

Ruth watched the pair stumble out of the living room, tumbling thumps and laughter echoing from the stairs as they chased each other up. While she waited for a quieting of the noise to tell her the upstairs landing was clear, Ruth, keen to be tucked up in bed with her ear plugs in, tidied the living room, loaded and set the dishwasher, wiped the kitchen surfaces.

In the weeks that followed, Ruth's empty days gave her both space and time to dwell upon the thoroughly diminished number of people in her life: her husband lost to that most terrible of clichés, for the middle aged woman at least, the younger model; her mother to dementia; her father dead years before, lost to that other terrible cliché, cancer. Her own lack of children, yet another character cliché, was always with Ruth, hidden from view as if tailing her in the blind spot of driving mirrors; she had to turn to get a proper look at the shape and speed of those particular regrets. To combat these disappearances and non-appearances, she submerged herself in the investigation of her mother's line, more than aware of what a vain, clutching attempt this was to fill both the time stretching out before her and the holes surrounding her where people should have been.

She noted dates, followed the thread of her family back across decades, the births, marriages and deaths bringing to mind the milestones of her own life: the day of her birth, the first chance meeting with the man who would become her husband, the day of their marriage, and every other day individualized by incidents in which she had taken some part. The thought came to her suddenly, when looking in the mirror and surprised by the pudging and lining of her own face, that there was yet another date, of greater importance to her than all those: that of her own death; a day which lay hidden and unseen among all the other days of the year, giving no sign or sound when she annually passed over it, but no less there, a shadow lurking behind the curtain. She wondered which day it was and why she did not feel the chill of each yearly encounter with it. Some time in the future, she realised, those who had known her would say: 'It is the day that poor Ruth Butterfield died', if indeed anyone noticed at all, yet that day remained unknown to her, would be unknowable until the very moment of its being, perhaps not even then. Almost at a leap, Ruth changed. Reflectiveness passed into her face, and a heavy note of regret at times into her voice. Her eyes grew larger and more prone to tears. Yet greater than all of this, a resolve grew inside her, as if readying her for something. She did not have to wait long to find out what.

Her vomiting in the mornings she first put down to stress, not thinking to check her diary for the date of her last period. They were not even close to regular at her age and the idea of pregnancy had been buried so far beneath the weight of her daily routine for so many years she had almost managed to forget the very concept. It was only upon throwing-up in the customer toilets of her local supermarket, that her thoughts coalesced into the idea of buying a pregnancy test. Leaving her trolley of shopping, Ruth grabbed a Clearblue from the amongst the feminine hygiene products and watched impatiently as the check-out conveyer crawled it towards the till.

Back in the toilets, the air still full of the stink of her sick, she squatted over a bowl and dipped the wand into the trickle of her urine. The action seemed ridiculous, a stupid, ugly thing to be doing, desperate and sad and pointless, but she did it anyway and waited until the wand read *Pregnant*. Only then, slumping back on the worn toilet seat, knickers round her knees, the strip lighting buzzing at her in reproof, did she allow herself to weep.

Ruth's maternal grandfather, long dead now himself, gave Ruth the leather-bound family Bible on her eighteenth birthday. The thick leather covering worn and faded, the wispy pages smelling of time and damp and something of the trees that had made them, the book seemed at once sturdy and delicate. Ruth turned immediately to the illuminated family tree inside the frontispiece of the large book and traced a finger over the gilt frames hanging from the branches and the names inscribed within. A number of the frames on her mother's side hung empty.

'I wouldn't look too deeply there,' her grandfather said, his hand over hers, gently pushing the book closed as he spoke. 'Some things are best left.'

Beyond that, the old man refused to be drawn. Ruth asked her mother what he had meant. Her mother looked elsewhere as she spoke.

'It's so long ago now it really doesn't matter.'

'If it doesn't matter then you can tell me,' Ruth said, but that argument wouldn't wash.

In the final, interminable nights of her mother's illness, Ruth had hoped her mother might relent. When, in a last moment of lucidity amidst the swirl of morphine-induced mumblings, she finally spoke as if in answer, Ruth thought it simply more gibberish, until she leaned in closer, the old woman's sour breath bearing the words weakly to her ear.

'I couldn't answer your questions. I couldn't ... I couldn't ... I couldn't answer your questions.'

Ruth stroked her hand. 'It doesn't matter, Mum. Don't upset yourself.'

'I don't know myself. I just don't know.'

'Don't know what, Mum?' Ruth pressed her ear almost to her mother's lips, could feel their movement.

'I don't know myself,' the old woman repeated then was silent.

It was these final words that had driven Ruth to begin the exploration of her mother's branch of the family tree, passively at first, watching television programmes in which celebrities explored their own family histories with varying degrees of success. In the early days of her grief this was all she could manage, sat in her armchair, supping cocoa from an oversized mug. She bought the book and DVD Rom supporting the series, and with a large photocopy of the Bible's family tree, her laptop and a broadband connection, she began to fill in the blanks as best she could.

Following Tessa's arrival, Ruth clung to this pursuit of her ancestors as if to an ally, and soon unearthed discoveries. Her mother giving birth to her at age eighteen was no surprise, but discovering the real date of her parents' marriage to be only four months before she was born rather than the sixteen she had been told did raise an eyebrow, much as it must have raised a few back in 1963. She found her grandmother and even her great-grandmother easily, both exactly when and where she expected them to be, and ordered copies of their birth certificates. It felt right to ascend this maternal line, as if in some way amends could be made for her own lack of offspring by following the line of mothers she had thought would end with her.

It was just days after the discovery of her middle-aged and very much unplanned pregnancy, that Ruth uncovered her great-great-great-grandmother. Just a name on her great-great-grandmother's birth certificate – *Mother: Nell Bryant nee Darch, Born: Alton Pancras in the county of Dorset, D.O.B: 10th August 1892.* The name niggled at Ruth in way she would have found difficult to describe had she anyone to tell. Perhaps this was the figure her grandfather and mother had been unwilling or unable to speak of. She entered the new details into the ancestry web form, hoping to find Nell there, but the search returned no matches.

Ruth decided to drive down to Dorset to see what she might uncover in the local archives and libraries. She travelled on a Sunday evening, staying overnight in a B&B to arrive at Dorchester Library at 9 a.m. prompt Monday morning for her appointment with a local historian. She did not tell her husband where she was going.

Malcolm Randall spoke with the hushed tones of someone who had spent many years working in quiet rooms. His appearance – a chubby boyish face topped with a ruffled thatch of blond hair, a brown suit, the same shade as his eyes, worn at the elbows and knees but not torn – somehow reassured Ruth.

'You'll be pleased to know that I managed to find Nell Darch's birth record.'

The historian beamed a proud little smile as he shook her hand and gestured to a chair. Together they sat and scanned the A3 copies of the Birth Register archive laid out upon the large reading table. The handwriting was difficult to read and she screwed her eyes to focus. The historian set a ruler under the relevant section of the record, but looked directly at Ruth as he spoke, the details memorised.

'Nell Darch; Born: 10th August 1892; Mother: Car Darch; Father: Unknown.'

She looked from him to the document, deciphering the swirls more readily now she knew what she was looking at, but saw nothing unusual in the name of her great-great-great-great-grandmother. For the next hour they attempted and failed to find any further record of her, either online or in the library archive. Nor could they find any clue in the documents as to the identity of Ruth's great-great-great-great-grandfather. Malcolm suggested Ruth check the library's newspaper archive while he investigated the parish records of the local churches.

'We can meet here same time tomorrow and compare notes,' he said.

Ruth spent the afternoon flicking microfiche pages across an antique screen, years flashing by with each turn of the wheel, her search revealing no birth announcement, no notice of engagement for Car Darch, nor any mention of the woman's name beyond the document the historian had given her.

She queried a librarian about her search. The young woman – they all seemed so young to Ruth now – led her to a quiet corner of the building and pulled down a magazine file stuffed with photocopied A5 booklets in folded card covers.

'Local history, amateur stuff, but you might find what you're looking for somewhere in here.' The librarian ran a finger along a shelf stocked with similarly-stuffed files. 'There's a load of them. Might take you a while.'

Ruth sat and piled the first collection of booklets on her right, taking each in turn and peeling back page after page of Xeroxed typewritten history interspersed with the odd poorly reproduced photograph. Finding no mention of Car Darch in the first stack, she refilled the magazine file, returned it to the shelf and selected a second and tried again. Then a third.

She was about to give up when, in a booklet about Dorset County Fairs of the late-nineteenth century, her eye came to rest on a poor quality photocopy of a faded photograph in which an Amazonian figure brandished a long-handled wooden mallet. The image would perhaps not have caught Ruth's eye for more than a moment but for the woman's facial features, which she recognised immediately as like her own. There was undoubtedly a strong resemblance, not least in the curve of the eyes and fullness of the cheeks, and the woman's hair, though unrestrained, almost wild, was of the same deep shade of black as Ruth's. They might, but for the intervening years, have been sisters.

The caption beneath the image named the woman as Car Darch. The text on the facing page described a typical Dorset county fair of the time, a line or two telling the story of the photograph. Apparently this Car Darch had bested a test-your-strength machine at one such fair, the force of her mallet blow shattering the mechanism in the process. Ruth looked again at the photograph. The woman's mane of dark hair tumbled over a surfeit of pale plump cleavage, the rolled sleeves of her blouse revealed muscular arms, the long fall of her black skirt fixed her to the ground, made her immovable and, most remarkably considering the grainy quality of the photocopy, the Amazon's eyes seemed both to greet Ruth and to challenge her.

On her way to the library exit, a photocopy of the photocopy of the photograph tucked into her document folder, Ruth noticed the Thomas Hardy display commemorating both his birthday and the 120th anniversary of the publication of his most celebrated novel. Picking up the commemorative edition from the display and using her driving licence as identification, she signed for a library card simply to borrow that one book.

Ruth first read *Tess* for A level at seventeen, back when her own story still lay open before her, the pages largely unwritten, the cover still bright, its corners not yet dog-eared, its spine not yet cracked and tired from use. She took little notice then of Car Darch, the Queen of Spades, her focus instead fixed firmly upon Tess and the terrible dilemmas Hardy forced upon the poor girl.

That evening, back at the B&B, Ruth opened the library copy and memories, not only of the book but also of who she herself was when she first read it, crowded the words on the page like marginalia. Reading the novel back then, flush with her own youth, it was easy to relate to Tess. Ruth herself had been desired and she had fretted over her own reputation and respectability, a concern fuelled by her mother's judgemental stare. It was only now, lying in her nightgown, her body, limbs, thoughts, feelings all so much more cumbersome than when she was seventeen, that she truly recognised Car Darch, and not only because the name appeared on her great-great-great-grandmother's birth certificate.

Ruth sat, her documents scattered across the bed, and scoured the pages of the novel for some mention of Car Darch being with child, but there was little mention of the character beyond the brief altercation with Tess in the early chapters. Instead Ruth rediscovered Tess's illegitimate child, Sorrow, the skimming of the pages bringing her all too quickly to the child's death and burial in that shabby corner of God's allotment where he lets the nettles grow, the grave marked with a cross fashioned from laths bound with string, and flowers in a marmalade jar.

Alone, in the rented room, Ruth curled up on the bed, clumsily cradled her warm belly with her cold palms and tried to sleep.

The next morning she showed the historian the novel.

'I'm afraid I've not read it,' Malcolm Randall said.

'Car Darch.' Ruth pointed at the copy of her great-great-great-grandmother's birth certificate. 'Car Darch.' She pointed at the name on a page in the novel.

Malcolm started to laugh but stopped as Ruth pushed the photocopy across the table to him.

'Car Darch,' Ruth said again, this time pointing to the caption.

He held the picture up and glanced from it to Ruth and back again.

'I'll admit there's a resemblance, but that doesn't mean the image in this photograph and the name on that birth certificate belong to the same person.'

Ruth, the novel still open in her hand, began to read.

'*To Tess's horror the dark queen began stripping off the bodice of her gown till she bared her plump neck, shoulders, and arms to the moonshine, under which they looked as luminous and beautiful as some Praxitalean creation, in their possession of the faultless rotundities of a lusty country girl. She closed her fists and squared up to Tess.*'

At the full stop she slapped the book shut and pointed at the photograph. 'Doesn't that sound like her?'

'If you're asking could this woman,' and here the historian tapped the photo of the woman wielding the mallet, 'be the sort to pick a fight with another, then I would say yes.'

'But what about the description, the plump neck, the sculpted frame? She's called dark Car because of her dark colouring. Her hair, for goodness' sake.' Ruth's voice rose and her fist clenched as she spoke. Malcolm took a step back before speaking again.

'Not everyone in Dorchester is an expert on Hardy, I'm

afraid. I certainly don't pretend to be. In fact I think it's fair to say we've reached the limit of my expertise.'

'You've found no record of her anywhere else?' Ruth said.

He shook his head. 'Nothing that predates her daughter's birth certificate. Mind, we are talking a long time ago and documents go missing, get destroyed. People fall through cracks.' The historian smiled, but Ruth couldn't stop thinking that Hardy's Car Darch, the Car Darch of the old photograph, and her Car Darch, mother to Nell and Ruth's own great-great-great-great-grandmother, were all one and the same.

'There might be someone who can help you,' said Malcolm, and without further explanation, he shuffled off into the library stacks.

Ruth scrabbled the novel open to her book-marked place and stared at the words on the page without reading them. On his return, the historian slid a month-old copy of the *Dorchester Echo* in front of her. Across the front page ran the headline *Hardy's Home Opens to the Madding Crowd*.

'There's a Hardy scholar in residence at Max Gate, working on a Ph.D, apparently.' In the picture of the house under the headline, a young woman stood at the front door smiling. 'Perhaps she can answer your questions.'

Max Gate stood at the end of a gravel path that circled a clump of rugged bushes before running up to the central arched porch of the front door. The red brick Victorian Villa, Ruth read in the newspaper article, was designed by Hardy himself, a trained architect by profession, if something other than poet and novelist were needed to describe him, and built by his brother and father. On a gloomier day it might have appeared foreboding, even Gothic, but that afternoon a bright sky and white clouds framed the gables and turrets and chimney pots, transforming the frown of its timber and tiles into a welcoming façade.

This was the house in which Hardy wrote *Tess* and *Jude* and hundreds of poems; the house he lived in for over forty years, growing to love it, despite reservations about its draftiness and the spiraling cost; the house Kipling, Stevenson, Sassoon, Shaw, Woolf, and Holst visited. Ruth gleaned all this from the article, but it was Car Darch that filled her thoughts as she hesitated just inside the gate, unwilling or unable to move closer to the property. Hearing a door unlatch, she looked across to the house in time to see the young woman from the newspaper article emerge from the shade of the arched porch. Ruth stood rooted in place as the woman smiled and crunched her way up the gravel path to the gate.

'You must be Ruth.' If the young woman's brilliant smile didn't announce her as American, her accent certainly did.

Ruth made to answer, but her eyes widened as no sound emerged. She stopped herself, attempted to start again, all the time aware of the young woman's eyes upon her. In front of this house and this stranger, Ruth could not hold the pieces of her own story together in anything approaching a narrative that someone else, someone so unfamiliar with her situation, might understand. The words choked inside her and Ruth could only watch as the young woman took her hand.

'I'm Andrea. I bet you'd love a cup of tea.'

Relieved, at least temporarily, of any need to explain, Ruth let herself be led inside.

They took tea in the conservatory, looking out across what

the young American called the middle lawn. Though she didn't usually indulge, Ruth agreed to sugar in her tea. She sipped at the sickly sweet beverage while Andrea looked over the birth certificate of Ruth's great-great-great-grand-mother and the photocopy of the photocopy of the pho-tograph. The student carefully unfolded the family tree, arranging the document on an antique table to inspect the branches closely. Ruth did her best to explain what had brought her to this place and the questions whirling about her head, omitting mention only of her pregnancy and her husband's infidelity.

'One thing jumps out.' Andrea pointed to the name on the birth register. 'The name Car is most likely short for something like Carol or Caroline, possibly Catherine, yet here, on the official record, just Car for the first name.'

Ruth leaned forward, her eyes fixed on Andrea.

'Looking at everything you've uncovered, the use of the name Car on the birth certificate suggests two possi-bilities. The first that Car was the woman's full name and Hardy, having met your ancestor, based his character upon her. The second that your ancestor is the actual fictional Car Darch somehow given life outside the novel.'

The idea dangled in the air before Ruth and she clung to it as if it were the bottom rung of a rope ladder she might use to climb out of herself, if only she could summon the strength to heave. Somewhere, at a distance, she heard Andrea give a little laugh.

'I think we can both agree that the first probability is the most likely.' Andrea picked up the photo. 'This one cer-tainly looks the part of dark Car. And she had an illegiti-mate child?'

Ruth nodded.

'Like Tess, but the child survived?'

Ruth nodded again.

'It might be, looking at this, that Hardy maybe took this woman's story and put his own tragic spin on it, kind of like when an author conflates two real people into a single character. Hardy perhaps took the events of your ancestor's life and transposed them to his character, Tess.' Andrea tapped the photo. 'If he took what happened to her and applied it to his maiden . . .'

Ruth went elsewhere as the young woman continued to speak. She saw Car Darch stood before her for a moment, bigger than, more beautiful than life.

'In all honesty though, Hardy probably never even met this woman. Perhaps he simply saw this photograph somewhere. Then there's always the possibility that the Car Darch in the photo simply isn't the one on the birth certificate.'

'But . . . but . . .' Ruth scrabbled, but the rung of the rope ladder was suddenly beyond her reach, rising as if attached to something lighter than air, and she felt too leaden to jump. The truth was that Ruth Butterfield – middle-aged, unhappily married, childless, parents deceased – had always felt like a supporting character in a story beyond her control. Arriving as it did, in the midst of so many other revelations, the possibility of a fictional character hiding a few generations back in the deepening branches of her family tree and to whom she was directly related had come as only a small shock. Indeed, it had quickly grown to be a notion that Ruth did not wish to part with.

'And the absence of the father's name is interesting. If your Car Darch was in fact the basis of Hardy's Car Darch and, in part, of Tess, we know what type of man he might well have been.'

The two women looked at each other. Ruth had been so focused on her Car Darch and Hardy's Car Darch that she had hardly considered the father.

'Your Car Darch recording the father as unknown might suggest that he were someone not a million miles away from Hardy's depiction of Alec D'Urberville.'

Ruth dropped her half-full teacup to the floor where it shattered. She stared at the china fragments at her feet. It was true, Hardy had not troubled his Car Darch with an illegitimate child, but certainly life had troubled her Car Darch with one, in a time when an illegitimate child spelt ruin. Ruth looked again at the Amazon in the photo, mallet in hand, ready to take on all comers. She imagined this woman, baby Nell in her arms, facing head-on a whole society that would judge her, condemn her. She imagined that strength flowing from mother to daughter, mother to daughter, a current channelling across the expanse of her family tree, something somehow new yet always inside her, waiting to be awakened. She felt it flood her. In the face of such a deluge, what did the quality of a father, known or unknown, matter?

These thoughts played themselves out in the confines of Ruth's imagining in the time it took for Andrea to retrieve a damp cloth from the kitchen.

'I'm so sorry,' Ruth said, collecting up the fragments of the cup, taking care not to cut herself upon the sharper pieces. She looked up from where she crouched over the damp patch in the rug. 'I know what to do.'

All too aware that the mess was of her own making, Ruth took the cloth and set about clearing it up.

～

She arrived home to find her key would not work in the lock. Before she could complain, the front door opened.

'Yes?' Tessa stood in the doorway, hands on her hips. Her hair, ponytailed with a red ribbon like a child's, drew attention, even more so than her Killers T-shirt, skinny jeans and high heels, to the fact that she wasn't as young as she liked to think.

Ruth barreled past, dragging her overnight bag behind, leaving Tessa to splutter and trail after, heels clacking on the wood effect flooring.

'Excuse me. Excuse me. You can't do that.'

Ruth parked her bag in the hall and headed for the kitchen. There she began clattering about in the cupboards, pulling out baking trays, a Tupperware pot of plain flour, a chunky brown mixing bowl she'd inherited from her mother.

On the drive back she had felt a craving for warm treacle tart like her mother used to make, and with the craving came a sudden and profound resumption of the grief she had managed to distract herself from. She wished for something of her mother to make it all better. By the time she pulled her car onto the drive she had resolved to follow her mother's recipe and make her own treacle tart.

'This is my house.' Ruth said, tipping flour into the bowl of her digital scale, her eyes fixed on the flickering numbers, her voice level and firm. 'I can do as I please in my own house.'

Tessa huffed and began tapping away at her mobile phone. Ruth rubbed the butter into the flour with her fingers, enjoying the greasy crumble of the mixture against her skin.

'Paul, it's me, she's turned up,' Tessa yapped into her phone. A pause. Then: 'No. You need to come home now.'

Another pause. Then: 'No. She's baking.' Another pause. 'Baking.' Another pause. 'No, I don't know what.'

'Treacle tart,' Ruth said without looking up. She heard Tessa snap her phone shut.

'He's on his way.'

Ruth expertly cracked an egg with one hand on the side of the bowl, dropping both white and yolk in before stirring them with a spatula.

'He's on his way, I said.'

Ruth lifted the dough from the bowl with one hand, sprinkled a light dust of flour onto the work surface with the other.

'He's very unhappy with you.'

Ruth kneaded the thick cloud of dough with her knuckles, squashed it with the heels of her palms.

'You can't live here anymore. Paul says.'

Ruth hoiked the lump of dough up and slapped it down again on the counter with a bang. Two steps took her to where Tessa was standing. Staring right at the younger woman, she reached without looking into the drawer next to her and pulled out a large wooden rolling pin.

'I said, this is my house.' Ruth raised the rolling pin, pointed the end at the tip of Tessa's nose. She held it there, a hair's breadth from touching, for just a moment before returning to the dough and beginning to roll it.

Ruth lined the loose-bottomed tart tin with the rolled dough, trimming the edge and pricking the base with a fork before stowing it on an empty shelf in the fridge to rest. Tessa huffed again as Ruth began work on the filling, crumbling a couple of slices of bread, zesting and juicing a lemon. She pulled the pot of ginger from the baking cupboard then stood confused for a moment.

'What have you done with the Golden Syrup?'

Ruth winced as the stupid girl began to giggle.

'It's up there.'

Ruth crossed the kitchen, opened the cupboard Tessa had pointed at, and retrieved the tin from the shelf. The lid was jammed on at an odd angle and syrup slid in tacky gloops down the side.

'It doesn't go there,' Ruth said.

Tessa tittered again. 'That's what I told Paul last night,' she said.

Ruth pulled a teaspoon from the cutlery draw and set about levering the lid from the tin. 'I beg your pardon.'

'I told Paul it doesn't go there.'

The titter was a full-blown giggle now. The lid refused to budge. Ruth heard Tessa say something about the syrup and bed sheets but was only half listening, her attention fixed on removing the battered lid. She gripped the tin firmly in one hand, pushing hard on the spoon with the other, her effort serving only to bend the handle. Grabbing a sturdy butter knife from the cutlery draw, she tried the lid again. Still it would not budge.

'I told him it'd be a right mess, but he insisted. Said he wanted to drizzle me in it and lick it all up.'

Ruth stabbed the knife under the lip of the lid again, wedging the thick blade in as far as possible.

'He said he could just eat me up.'

A broad, hefty grunt, something like a calfing cow, burst from deep inside Ruth and she flung her fist high above her head, slamming it down on the fat handle of the knife. For just a flash of thought she imagined her fist as a mallet. The force of her blow jettisoned the lid into the air and pulled the tin from her hand after it, the syrup spurting from the wide hole splattering Ruth's face and hair, slopping over her top. She grabbed at the tin, her fingers tripping over each other. As it bounced from her fingertips, she lurched forward to snatch it, slipped and fell to the floor, the tin clattering after her, spewing the last of the syrup as it rolled lazily on the tiles beside her.

Ruth groaned a little where she lay. Rubbing syrup from her eyes, she raised herself to a sitting position, wiped the worst from her face with her fingers and looked up at Tessa, who had not moved from her spot by the fridge. As the piercing volley of Tessa's laughter burst from her smirking mouth, Ruth's long smouldering sense of injustice finally inflamed her to action. She sprang to her feet and closely faced the object of her scorn.

'How dare you laugh at me, hussy!' she cried.

'I can't help it,' Tessa blurted between bursts of laughter.

'You think you're better than me because you're his new model now. But stop lady, stop right there. I'm as good as two of you.' Ruth yanked her syrup-smeared cardigan and blouse over her head, the vest top she wore beneath revealing her plump neck, shoulders, and arms. Picking up the rolling pin, her ample bosom rising and falling in time with her heavy exhalations, she squared up to Tessa.

'I'm not looking for a fight.' Tessa had stopped laughing now and was backing up a step or two.

'Too late,' Ruth said following her retreat, forcing her further down the hall.

'Don't come near me.'

Tessa pulled frantically at the lock, her eyes fixed on Ruth marching down the hall towards her, rolling pin in hand. Tessa flung the door open and staggered out onto the drive and Ruth followed, stopping on the front step, her hands on her hips, the lusty maturity of her frame in the late afternoon sun suddenly as radiant and formidable as some Lachaiseian sculpture.

Tessa was retreating further up the drive when a BMW convertible, its top down, pulled up with a scream of brakes and horn. Paul Butterfield hoisted himself from the driver's seat.

'What the devil is all this row about?' He looked first to Ruth then, when no answer was forthcoming, to Tessa, who, on cue, burst into tears.

'Let's get you in the car,' he said, wrapping an arm around her shoulder and leading her to the passenger side. 'I promise we'll soon be shot of this stupid cow.'

With Tessa inside the car, he crossed the drive to face Ruth.

'You're a bloody disgrace,' he said, his face as close to hers as his short stature allowed. Small flecks of spit fired from his fat lips. 'Look at the state of you. My solicitor will be hearing about this.'

Ruth felt almost ready to faint, so vivid was her sense of this crisis. At almost any other moment she might have ignored his abuse, as indeed she had refused to anger at his poor treatment of her so many times before; and now the hurt she felt would not of itself have forced her to do otherwise. But coming as these insults did at the particular juncture when embarrassment over her being covered in syrup and fears about her future could be transformed by a swing of a fist into a triumph over both, she abandoned herself to her impulse, dropped the rolling pin to the floor, squared up to her soon-to-be-ex-husband, and, with her right fist, walloped him smack in the chops, knocking him flat upon his back.

The pair were speeding away in a furious cloud of exhaust fumes by the time Ruth was properly aware of what had happened. She forgot the stickiness of the syrup in her hair and on her skin and simply stood at the door of her reclaimed home, her gaze fixed in the direction of the convertible's whine as it shrank into silence up the road.

'You all right, Ruth?' asked a neighbour who had stepped from her front door too late to witness the incident. 'What was all that noise?'

'I'm fine,' Ruth said. 'Sorry Jean, I have to be getting back inside, I've something in the oven.'

With that she turned and went back to her kitchen, laughing to herself, her right hand gently stroking her belly.

IT'S A COUPLE OF COATS COLDER UP THERE

I built the house on the mountain for just that reason. The cold sweeps across the flank of land I picked up at auction for a song, chilling anything standing on it, making warm blood run cold.

Not that yours needed help. You suffered in even the slightest chill. Layers of clothing, thrown on to combat the cold, would hide you away, yet in some perverse diminishing return, the more physically cold you were, the less physically remote you became. Your fingers, daggers of ice in cold weather, would seek me out, your hands shoving under my fleece, under my T-shirt, until shivering palms were nestled on the curve of my stomach.

You loved the view from here, helped design the house, plan the garden. We made space for children, should they come along, an annex for family to stay. The space we had to build was all the excuse we needed.

That first night, huddled together before the ostentatious fireplace you insisted upon, I begged forgiveness for forgetting the matches. There would be no fire tonight. We fetched blankets and duvets from the moving boxes and huddled upon the sofa.

Your fingers found my belly, seeking only warmth, but allowing me the contact I craved.

'I'll warm you up,' I said.

IMPACT

The moment the sound becomes audible, Sam is dragging his feet to school, swinging his rucksack back and forth over the rough path through the field behind his house. A light in the sky burns towards him and the noise blossoms into a sustained boom that threatens to crack the sky. The meteorite, for that is what Sam later discovers it is, strikes him, slicing a scar into the back of his hand before knocking him down. He lands, dazed and utterly alive, staring at the pea sized rock that sits in a foot wide crater punched into the ground.

Years from now, Sam will hold his wife's hand and weep. He will cling to the weak pulse that resonates from palm to palm, squeezing tighter as if doing so will keep the old woman from leaving. It is then Sam's eyes will alight on his childhood scar and he will marvel that the impact of this moment hurts in so many more ways than his collision, so long ago, with a nugget of rock that fell upon him from space.

RUBIK'S CUBED

The original cubes you could dismantle into component parts, revealing the inner workings before slotting and clicking the colours back into place, bypassing the entire puzzle in favour of the purely mechanical effort of assembling the coloured sides. It was an exercise in reconstruction rather than revelation, destroying something to rebuild it as it should be, all parts perfectly in place without the hard work.

The new ones, smaller than the ones of my youth, though my larger hands might create this illusion, probably work the same way, the partial cubes that make up individual face colours backed with an almost-arrowhead of plastic to slot and grip in the central stems around which the rows and columns shift when wrenched this way and that.

We sit on opposite sofas and I try to make sense of what you tell me. You explain what has gone wrong for you and I slot that into place with the reasons you give for why we can't go on like this. I twist the puzzle of our relationship around in my head, but it is impossible to keep track as you throw more colours into the mix. Somehow the cube has more than six sides, colours have been added beyond the traditional red, white, blue, yellow, green and orange. The rows and columns increase in size to accommodate the added purple and pink, grey and brown and more.

'We can work this out,' I say, my mind twisting and turning what you have said further and further into disorder.

'There's nothing to work out,' you say.

I look at your bags, packed and ready at the door, and realise the puzzle is already in pieces and no matter how hard I push it won't fit back together.

THE BUS SHELTER

Nursing homes are using a novel strategy to stop Alzhei-mer's patients from wandering off: phantom bus stops ... They know the bus sign and remember that waiting there means they will go home.

—Fake bus stop keeps Alzheimer's patients from wandering off
Daily Telegraph, 3 June 2008

It's first thing in the morning, bright sunlight streams through the window and Willard wants to go home. He has lived in the care home for some months now, the furniture and decor of his room clean but dated, yet the room is unfamiliar to him. More and more often these days he forgets where he is or where he is going, his mind abandoning him in a corridor or another patient's room with no memory of how he came to be there or why. Today though, Willard's desire to go home, like the early morning sun outside, manages to break through the clouds surrounding it.

He puts on his brown suit, the last he bought before he retired. It fits him well despite the intervening years. Taking great care to get it just right, Willard knots his tie the way Dad taught him; the memory of his father as clear in his mind as if it were yesterday. His age-worn fingers cross, loop and pull with great care. Using both hands, Willard tightens the perfect Windsor knot and draws it up to his collar.

Smoothing down his lapels, Willard's head fills with how his mother kissed him on the cheek every morning as he left for work. Sixteen years old, his first proper job, junior salesman in a department store selling electricals. She would give him his lunch and peck his cheek as he left by the kitchen door. This was before he married Jeanie from down the road, before they moved to the flat in town, before the twins and Carol were born, before Jeanie died and Willard got old. But Willard cannot recall those things today. This morning his head is filled with Mum and Dad.

He remembers the house he shared with his parents. The number seven bus ran down Wingate Street and he would catch it with Mum and Pauline, the three of them heading into town for a matinee at the Odeon. Willard would race his sister to the stop, their shoes clattering on the paving slabs, Mum calling them, telling them to slow down. Willard knows if he can get into town he can catch a number seven and he can get home. He checks his pocket for change and sets off.

This early in the morning most of the staff have yet to arrive for the day shift, making it easy for Willard to slip out unnoticed. He instinctively avoids the lobby area and leaves through a side door left open by a laundry delivery man taking a cigarette break. No one sees Willard crunch his way down the gravel drive. His eyes dart about, looking for one thing, and finding it he breaks into a shuffle; the closest he gets to a run these days.

The bus shelter outside the gates is a shiny, new construction, like a wooden shed with one side missing and a well-made bench built into the interior. The roof canopy protects those waiting for a bus from the rain. Willard absently jingles the coins in his trouser pocket as he moves toward the bus stop. If he waits, a bus is sure to come.

Like the shelter, the sign is new. The crisp red, white and blue of the bus company logo reminds Willard of the Union Jack bunting that decorated houses in the street parties of his youth. His parents would dance and sing while someone played an upright piano moved from a neighbour's front parlour. Willard ran with the other children of Wingate Street, waving flags and laughing. There was jelly and ice-cream and lemonade to drink. Sitting on the bus stop bench, Willard smiles, safe inside memories of victory celebrations and coronations and jubilees.

The sun continues to pierce the grey sheet of cloud above. He removes his jacket and folds it carefully across his knee so as not to crease it. A bird sings somewhere in the canopy of trees lining the quiet road and Willard cocks his head and listens. A breeze rustles the trees, abruptly ending the birdsong, sending the bird skyward. Willard watches it leave then looks at the bus stop sign and a wave of perplexity washes across his face. Then the number seven bus and his desire to go home slip back into view.

Seven was also the number of the house on Wingate Street, his home for the first nineteen years of his life; a red brick terrace on an estate of red brick terraces. As a young man, the familiarity of the streets was comforting. He knew who he was and people knew him. Willard was Alice-from-number-seven's boy who married a local girl and ended up working in the same office for nearly forty years.

Willard could murder a cup of tea now, with two sugars, just like his mum used to make him after work. Willard likes sugar in his tea again now. He doesn't remember that he stopped taking sugar in the first year of his marriage.

Jeanie didn't take sugar and always forgot to put any in his. In this way, like so many others, his taste synchronised to hers as their married life progressed. Until he lost her twice; first to cancer, and then to his declining memory. Now all he wants is a cup of hot sweet tea from his mother's china pot.

As a very small boy he would wait at the bus stop at the end of the road for his father to come home from work. The number seven would arrive just after five and twenty past five and Dad would stride off the bus, hoist Willard up onto his broad shoulders and the pair would rush home for a game of football in the yard. The game always descended into rough and tumble. Dad would pin him down to tickle him, laughing as Willard roared and screamed and loved every second, Mum calling them in when tea was on the table. Sat on the bus stop bench, his jacket folded over his knees and suddenly very tired, Willard listens for his mother's voice.

It isn't her voice he hears but the dull roar of an engine. Looking up Willard sees the double-decker make its way down the street, a cloud of smoke trailing from the exhaust. The green paint of the bus is faded and not at all the colour of the local buses these days. Willard smiles when he sees the number and stands, holding his arm out to tell the driver to stop. It pulls closer and Willard sees his father at the doors, ready to alight.

'There you are, Willard.'

The voice from behind is not his father's. Willard turns to see a young man in a pale uniform, smiling and speaking softly. 'It's a beautiful day.'

'I want to go home,' Willard says, 'The bus is here.'

The young man steps slowly closer. 'There's no bus for at least an hour,' he says taking Willard gently by the arm,

'Come inside and we'll get you a cup of tea. We can come back later.'

Willard looks back up the street, but the bus is gone. 'Cup of tea?' he says.

'And biscuits.'

Willard has no memory of it, but he has been found at the bus stop many times before, sitting safely on the polished bench waiting for a bus that can never come. Once again and for the first time, he allows himself to be led away from the stop, all thoughts of home drifting silently into the clouded corners of his mind. As the crunch of his footsteps on the gravel drive merge with those of the care assistant, Willard wonders what biscuits he will have today.

BODY OF EVIDENCE

I used to believe my husband when he said he was working late. But that was before Mum rang to say she'd seen him with a blonde woman outside the Park Hotel. I said she was likely just a colleague, he was likely just giving her a lift, it was likely something and nothing. I was wrong. Mum saw them kissing.

'It's a disgrace, him up to all sorts and you about ready to drop,' she said.

Now when he comes home late, I pretend to be asleep. I listen to him shower. I wait for him to climb into bed. Only once he's sleeping do I turn and ask, 'Where were you between the hours of 6 p.m. and 11 p.m. tonight? Who were you with? How long has this been going on?' He doesn't answer. He sleeps too deeply. He's tired from a hard day's work and whatever else he's been up to. But I have other methods of investigation.

Procedure is important. There must be reasonable suspicion: circumstances strong enough to justify a prudent and cautious person's belief that certain facts are probably true. Even hearsay – if it is from a reliable source – can form the basis for reasonable suspicion. As for motive, I only have to look in a mirror, at my bloated face, at the hardboiled egg of my belly, at the stretch marks raking the skin of my thighs and torso, at the swell of my feet and ankles and legs, to see why he might go elsewhere. His work provides opportunity.

My file has dates and times going back to when Mum informed on him: the evenings he was late home; weekend seminars in Birmingham and Reading, Luton and Manchester. I've collated the names of those attending and whittled them down to two or three possible suspects, but a good brief will assert such evidence is merely circumstantial and implies no real wrong doing. So I let him scurry back into our bed without challenge and when I am sure he is sleeping, careful to be quiet, careful not to wake him, I gather the last shreds of proof.

Last night I collected hairs from a shirt he'd balled up in the washing basket. Three long blonde strands, one stuck to the shoulder, one curled half in the breast pocket, a third trailing down the shirt back. All three are bagged and safe inside the A4 case file under my desk. Still, even this is not enough to convince a judge or a jury of his peers. That will require harder evidence.

The fact of our own relationship, despite our recent problems, is supported by just such evidence. Our marriage is beyond reasonable doubt. Even if there were no marriage certificate (and there is) or witnesses to the ceremony (and there are), there is Exhibit A, my heavily pregnant self. The baby elbowing my insides is an irrefutable DNA record of our marriage. Hard evidence of a sexual relationship. A witness to the fact of love between two people. The full extent of this other woman's relationship to my husband remains unclear.

Following him is not an option. In my condition I tire quickly and am hardly built for stealth. Then there's the frequency with which I have to pee. Fortunately, having his iCloud password makes tracking him via his phone's location settings a cinch. I keep the Find My iPhone map tabbed in my browser and track him through the day, the phone's green dot hovering over his office before circulating the various branches scattered about the area he manages. I pay particular attention when he calls to say he's working late, watching the dot leapfrog streets with each page refresh, moving across town in nearly real time, always ending up in the same street at the same house. In Google Maps' satellite view, I squint at the cars parked along the tree-lined cul-de-sac in the hope it might give me some clue about how long this has been going on, but the resolution is too low to tell if one is his. I drive by the house, but during the day there's no one there, just empty bay windows with pretty curtains, a well-tended garden and an empty space at the kerb outside. I take photos for the file anyway.

This evening, when he texts to say he will be home late, I am already parked down the street from the house. I have a Thermos of coffee, a blanket over my lap and my camera on the dashboard. I see his car first. It pulls to the kerb alongside the front garden. Her Audi continues past him and pulls onto the drive. I am already taking photographs when she steps from the car. Her tall, slim frame is elegant in a dark trouser suit. Her legs are long. Her blonde hair trails down her back. Her smile is a polished white. There is nothing sleepless, tired, or heavy about her. I see their figures in miniature through the viewfinder of my camera, see him smile as he beeps his car and steps to her. They are kissing before they are even through the door. I wait for a while to see if there is anything worth photographing through the windows, but they are busy elsewhere in the house. Eventually I go home and wait.

When he finally gets home, I lie still and listen for the

shower, but he doesn't turn it on, just staggers in, drops his clothes beside the bed, and climbs in. I smell whisky and wonder if he has driven himself home; another charge to add to the list, perhaps. I have been waiting for a night like tonight. His unwashed body is a crime scene. He is dirty with evidence. The stink of her still hangs on him. There will be fibres and DNA and fingerprints in his car, on his clothes, stuck to his skin. I check his clothes first and find more blonde hairs, further confirmation, then I pull out the fingerprint kit stowed in my bedside drawer.

Fingerprints are the impression left by the epidermal ridges of human fingers. Epidermal ridges amplify sensation when fingertips brush a surface, increasing the quality of signals transmitted to the sensory nerves involved in fine texture perception. They also improve the gripping of both rough and smooth wet surfaces. Prints themselves are composed of natural secretions, most typically sweat from the eccrine glands in the ridged skin of the fingertips, but any material on the friction ridges will also be transmitted to the surface touched. The substances most often found in fingerprints are sweat, oil, grease, ink, blood, vaginal secretions and semen.

A host of factors can interfere with the lifting of a clear print: the pliability of the suspect's skin, deposition pressure, slippage, the composition of the surface material. It is important not to pour the powder directly from the jar onto the surface being investigated. Too much powder will contaminate the prints. Enough can go wrong in the forensic process without creating problems.

I sprinkle the dust lightly, my kit open on the bed beside me, the pony-hair brush clamped in my teeth. Uncovering an image of her fingertips will feel like understanding:

who she is, why he sees her, how we are different, how we are the same.

I take the first print from his cheek. Evidence of a caress? The second from his upper arm. A friendly squeeze or passionate embrace? The print upon his naked skin suggests the latter. The third, taken from the inner thigh of his right leg, seems evidence enough to convict. I am about to gather up the prints, creep downstairs to my desk and add them to the file, when the pull of the tape as I lift the last print wakes him. He sees the kit on the bed, the clouds of powder on the sheets, on his skin. He sees the brush still gripped in my teeth, the white cards stuck with tape bearing the dark swirls of his co-respondent's prints.

'What the hell?' he says.

I pull the brush from between my teeth, point it at him, look him hard in the eye.

'I'll ask the questions,' I try to say but can't. The first contraction stops the words and the breath to speak them. I turn my eyes to his and see that he understands. The mix of fear and wonder in his face makes it impossible to say if he will stay or run.

THE MAN WHO
LIVED LIKE A TREE

The man who lived like a tree did so at first without realising. Growing tall and broad, he married his childhood sweetheart and started a family, sinking his roots deep into the earth. For each of those early years, a ring grew inside him, thick with love. That is, until his wife began to age when he did not; then brittle, leaf-thin rings began to widen the space between his heart and skin in fragile increments.

'Look at you, still so handsome,' his wife would say.

'And you, still so beautiful,' he would reply, each time lifting her hand, light-boned as a bird's wing, in his hand, sturdy as an oak branch, kissing it and wishing that she could stay with him or he move on with her, but that was not the life nature planned for them. Instead, the man who lived like a tree spent days stood beside the bed where she lay dying, his sunken heart throbbing in his trunk, his large frame throwing a canopy of cooling shade across her like a soft blanket as the sound of their grandchildren at play burst through the window hand-in-hand with the bright summer sun.

For years after her death he did little but play with his

grandchildren, spending hours in the garden chasing and being chased.

'Granddad, why do you not grow older like Mummy or Daddy?' Eleanor, his most beloved grandchild, asked one day as they sat on the grass together.

'I don't know,' said the man who lived like a tree.

'Will you still be young when I am old?'

He swept the girl into the carved muscles of his arms, swung her up to the bough of his shoulders, her laughter ringing with echoes of her grandmother.

'I sincerely hope not,' he said.

Decades passed and the man who lived like a tree watched Eleanor lowered into the earth, just as he had watched his wife and too many children, too many grand-children before her. He tried to recall whose child it was, fresh-faced and full of spring, that took his arm and led him back to the funeral car, tried to remember what branch connected them across the span of years, but generations had added too many fruits to his family to count and his thoughts were slower now, more gradual in their motion. He could no more grasp the answer than leaves can touch the wind.

Often now he wept and wished for the day when his roots, no longer nourished by the fast moving world, would shrivel and shrink in the earth, the weight of his years top-pling him, finally, to the ground.

'I am so very old,' he said to his family of strangers, but they were too young and fast and busy to really hear.

And so it was, until some years later, stood in the garden he so loved, face turned to the sun, the toes of his bare feet splayed in the grass, and with a final sorrowful ring wrap-ping itself around the core of him, he finally, happily felt his roots fail. The family laid him to rest at the bottom of the garden just as the auburn rush of autumn filled the trees.

The following spring a sapling thrust from the soil under which he lay. Years passed and the sapling grew, adding ring after ring of cambium beneath its crust of bark. By the time it was firmly established there was no one left who remembered the man who had lived like a tree.

A young girl, so many generations removed from him yet directly related all the same, spent hours climbing amongst the mature branches. One bright spring morning, clambering amongst new leaves freshly broken from their buds, she called down to her parents to come and see.

'There are names on the leaves,' she told her mother and father, who fetched a ladder to look.

Written in the impossible venations of each leaf was a name, each one different as each leaf is different; every one a son or daughter, grandson or granddaughter of the long forgotten man, generation after generation after generation unfolding and branching and budding in fresh leaves as the family continued to grow up and out and into the sky.

THINGS I NO LONGER
WISH TO POSSESS

In no particular order and by no means exhaustive:

A vague sense of dissatisfaction that clings to me like stink. Mask it all I can with deodorants and colognes, it finds its way to my nostrils, penetrates me where I breathe.

The sofa I can't throw away. In the years since we squeezed the leather behemoth in here, I swear it's gained mass. Its girth dwarfs the door frame's width now, and even if it did fit, I've done the maths, the thing would never swing the hall corner and out the front door without jamming. I would chop it up but the thing still bears the scar of my last attempt, a jagged slice cut inches into the back rest as far as I got. I swear it screamed as I powered the blade back and forth, back and forth through its remarkable solidity.

Your old toothbrush, splayed bristles felled like trees in a tornado, kept in the utility room, stuffed under the sink, ready to clean dog shit from the maze print of my sneaker should the need arise.

The artificial tree lurking in the attic like a mad woman

waiting to be assembled and dressed, let out only for the holidays.

Your contempt. The only piece of you left behind. Somehow visible every time I look in the mirror.

The pockets of household refuse planted in the yard like dirty time capsules. When things are really bad I think about exhuming them, as if holding a yoghurt pot or tin can still wearing your fingerprints might make things better.

THIRD PARTY,
FIRE & THEFT

The car burns as I sleep fully reclined in the driver's seat. The acrid plastic smoke wakes me. The smell of burning dolls.

A crowd clatters out from the cliff-top café next to the tourist car park, the cook banging a thick fist on the driver side window. Smoke curls its heavy weather system about my head as he tugs frantically at the handle of the locked car door.

I jab the button with the white lock symbol in the driver's side armrest and nothing happens. Nothing happens. Nothing happens.

The driver side window pelts me with artificial hail. Two hands find me, scrunch me up in my jacket and yank me through the hole where the window used to be.

The cook props me against the pay and display machine, sits with me to wait for the emergency services. We watch the fire spread across the car. The heat blows the remaining glass and the fire stretches out from the windows to claw the sky, smoke thick as blood trailing into the air from its fingertips.

A whole cutback-proposal's worth of emergency service

professionals tell me I am lucky to be alive. Multiple firemen. Two paramedics. Three police officers, one of them a woman who holds my hand like my mother used to.

I relax against the pay and display machine and watch the firemen hose the car back under control, its blackened frame fizzing and popping like a broken soda stream as the water hits.

The policewoman is first to ask the question. We're going over how the fire started and both acknowledge that I might have died. She crouches down in front of me, her face filled with the distance of someone waiting to say what they are thinking rather than listening to what is being said.

'Let's go back to before the fire started,' she says. 'What were you doing sleeping in the car?'

I can't help thinking the answer is in the question.

In the hospital, the orderly wheeling me to the ward talks about a car he owned once, the windscreen of which repeatedly and spontaneously shattered. He blamed local youths with their ASBOs and hooded jumpers, until it happened again as he walked across the hospital car park toward the car. He tells me the glass buckled and flexed, as if squeezed by some invisible giant fist, before shattering onto the front seats.

I spend the afternoon waiting for a doctor to discharge me, hooked up to an oxygen mask, breathing air that smells like the inside of blister packaging. The TV bolted to the wall near the ceiling plays property programmes at an inaudible volume. A lesbian couple is being shown round a series of houses for sale, each one more expensive than the last.

A middle-aged woman sleeps in the bed beside me, hooked to a drip that beeps in alarm every so often. Each time a nurse scurries in with a different sized, different coloured plastic sack of fluid to string from the stand.

'The doctor will be with you soon,' the nurse says each time she exits past my bed, folding the empty fluid bag like a crisp packet.

The forms start with my being discharged. The doctor says my exposure to the smoke was minimal. There is no need for further observation. My disappointment at hearing this tastes the same as that which hit me when overlooked for a role in the school play as a child.

I walk back to the car park on the cliff and stare at the scorch marks on the tarmac. Cars park either side once more, but no driver braves placing their car over the burnt space. I wait and watch two or three cars approach, the drivers considering the gap, rolling down their windows for a closer look at the burn marks before continuing the hundred yards or so down the road to the next short-stay car park.

I fish my phone from my pocket and take photos of the empty space.

Police reports and insurance forms describe the fire as 'fully engaged'. The policewoman and the claims adjustor repeat the phrase in their questions. The newspapers prefer words like *blaze* and *conflagration* and, in one particularly striking headline, *inferno*.

I write down my version in the clearest language I can, squeezing events into the box frames and pre-drawn lines of the various forms. I stick to a clear past tense and words that generate the least amount of ambiguity when placed together. The process reminds me of writing a 'What I did on my holidays' composition for the start of school term.

The claims adjustor calls round to clear up a few details. She wears a trouser suit and clicks her silver ballpoint in and out three times before writing anything on her forms. I sign my name with her pen, clicking it in and out to steady myself.

At the door, she says, 'We'll be in touch if we have any further questions.'

She returns later that week.

'It seems there is some irregularity in how the fire started,' she says, clicking the pen in and out before ticking something off the list on her lap. 'It seems the police and fire forensic teams have been unable to ascertain the cause of the fire.'

I watch the ballpoint of the pen, a tiny smudge of black ink squatting on the silver bullet of it, flick in and out three times. She crosses through something on her list.

'Could you tell me what you remember?'

'I was sleeping.'

'Why was that?'

'I was tired.'

'Do you often sleep in cars parked on cliff-top car parks?'

'Only my own.'

The cheek of my response tastes of strawberries.

'You will understand that we simply cannot authorise a claim on your policy if there is any question of irregularities in the events surrounding the fire.'

'I will, yes,' I say, enjoying myself.

She shuffles her papers together. 'We'll be in touch,' she says.

I miss out a lot of incidental details when filling in the spaces on the claim forms, some true and some not so. If I list them, which is which should become clear.

Before I fell asleep there was someone else in the car with me. Had the passenger seat not burned along with the rest of the car a faint indentation in the upholstery may well have been visible to the trained eye of the forensic investigators.

I dreamt of fire while I slept. A circle of fire around which a camp had been struck. Trees shielded the clearing from the wind and music played from somewhere above. I sat alone, looking up at the stars, each one a furnace reduced to a pin-prick in the dark fabric of the sky. Then the smell and sound and reality of the burning car yanked me awake.

My older brother gave me the car. He handed me the keys before leaving for his new job. 'Take care of it,' he said. 'Don't go driving it off a cliff.'

I had fallen asleep staring at the sea.

I had fallen asleep crying.

I had fallen asleep crying at the sea.

I had fallen asleep fully engaged.

My passenger, the one whose indentation in the passenger seat forensic investigators might have found, told me something before he got out of the car. 'Things are never as bad as they seem,' he said. Or was it, 'It's always darkest before the dawn'? Or was it, 'Chin up, it might never happen'?

Sat propped against the cold metal of the pay and display machine, I watched as the car became a signal pyre, warning passing vessels of danger. I felt the threat in my throat, thick and choking like the smoke I inhaled. I warmed my hands on the heat of its warning.

When the claims adjustor returns, she brings a policewoman with her. The same one who held my hand on the day of the fire. How's that for coincidence?

'Witnesses have described a third party in the car with you,' the policewoman says.

'That is reassuring. I was beginning to think I'd imagined him.'

They both stare at me.

'See, she gets snarky and uncooperative when questioned,' the insurance investigator says.

'It is in your best interests to cooperate fully with our inquiries.' The policewoman reaches forward and takes my hand as she says this.

'It's been such an ordeal,' I say.

The claims adjustor glares at me over a fresh pile of forms, clicking and un-clicking her pen, but unable to cross out anything on the list in front of her.

The car saved my life. Or falling asleep did. Or both. What I might have done had I woken in the car to find it not burning is a mystery, an intangible other-worldly alternative of quantum physics. Somewhere I woke or never slept at all, turned the ignition and drove the car into the sea, the body work spiraling off like orange peel as it bounced down the cliff side. Or I woke and drove home and had a cup of tea. Or glass of milk. Or just sat and stared at the sea.

Except none of that happened. Or all of it did.

What I didn't tell the police is this. I drove the car to the cliff car park, though the cliff isn't so much a cliff as a tall hill leading away from the beach, landscaped to prevent erosion that has eaten away at this coastline dramatically since the seventies. I sat there imagining the sea taking a big bite of the coast, sucking in the car and me with it. I felt the water fill the inside, pressure squeezing me into my seat as I sank to the sea bed.

I closed my eyes and only opened them again when the

car door opened. I had left the doors unlocked. Beside me sat a young man with wild eyes. He was staring right at me and smiling.

'Can I have this?' he said and tapped a grimy finger on the dash above the car stereo.

I nodded.

'Thanks.'

He pulled a large screwdriver from the pocket of his combats and set about wrenching the stereo out of its socket.

'Didn't mean to scare you,' he said. As he worked, he gripped his tongue in his teeth in that way that men do when they concentrate.

'You didn't,' I said.

'Only you looked a little startled.' He ripped the stereo free with a screech as he said this.

'Did I?'

He tugged out the cables that connected the stereo to the car and grinned.

'A little.'

He placed the screwdriver back in his pocket and held the stereo unit with both hands as if checking the weight.

'Thanks for this,' he said, opening the door to get out.

I spoke the words before I thought them.

'Could you stay for a bit?'

He looked at me for a moment.

'Just until I fall asleep?'

He looked at the stereo and then at me.

'Seems fair enough,' he said.

We sat and listened to the sea chewing at the beach below.

The police fail to find a cause for the fire. Though it started somewhere under the dashboard, faulty wiring is ruled out. They ask about the missing car stereo, but I tell them it didn't have one. Arson, in the absence of any evidence to the contrary, is also dismissed as a possible cause.

'Act of God,' the claims adjustor says.

'God? Really?'

'You realise what this means?'

I nod and sign the forms, happy for it all to be over.

I am required to pay for the disposal of the car.

'I think I'll have it back,' I say.

The police and the claims adjustor have the same nervous look in their eyes when I tell them this.

'What do you intend to do with it?' they both enquire. I don't say and they give up asking. In the end, I think they're happy to be rid of me.

I pay a local garage to collect the car.

'Are you sure you want it here?' the tow-truck driver says, climbing about on the flat bed, unfastening the thick grey safety straps from the car, readying it to be winched down from the truck. 'You'll get done for abandoning a vehicle.'

I watch the car slide down the ramp, amazed that the wheels, tyres melted into formless black, still turn. The car, once canary yellow, is now patterned in blacks and bronzes and flashes of white, the path the flames took visible in the melting of plastic, the blistering of paint, the discoloura-tion of metal.

'I'm not abandoning it,' I say.

I wait for the tow truck to pull away before climbing in behind what remains of the steering wheel. The ravaged stump of the driver's seat presses uncomfortably into my thighs as my stare passes through the windscreen, over the cliff and into the sea below.

ULTRASOUND I

The tapping was the first sign that there was something unusual about Rebecca's pregnancy. It started in her twelfth week, light fingered taps deep inside her. At first she thought they were hiccups, but her pregnancy book told her that at twelve weeks the baby's lungs would not yet be developed enough to hiccup, and anyway, the tapping went on far longer than hiccups should.

She told her husband, Tony, who shrugged his shoulders and suggested she ask the midwife.

'It's certainly early to be feeling anything like that,' the midwife said as she readied the foetal doppler to listen to the baby's heartbeat.

Rebecca lifted her top and the midwife squirted ultrasound gel onto her belly, the chill of it setting off another bout of tapping.

'It's happening now,' Rebecca said, sitting up.

'Lie back, honey, and let's see what's going on,' the midwife said, easing Rebecca back onto the examination bed.

The midwife stroked the doppler probe across her skin, the speaker crackling with Rebecca's belly gurgles. The galloping hoof-beat of the baby's heart buzzed from the speaker and the midwife jotted the rate down in Rebecca's notes. She whirled the doppler probe one final time and that was when she found it.

Taaap. Tap tap tap tap. Tap taaap. Taaap. Pause. *Taaap tap taaap tap. Taaap taaap taaap. Tap taaap tap tap. Taaap tap tap.*

The midwife looked worried, but pasted a smile on her face.

'I'll just get the doctor.'

Rebecca waited in the exam room alone, wishing Tony had asked for time off work to come with her. The midwife returned with the doctor and they listened again to the heartbeat and then to the tapping. The doctor listened, eyes wide with impossibility.

'It's Morse Code,' he said. 'It seems the baby doesn't like the cold of the gel.

The ultrasound scan confirmed it. In the picture Rebecca took home, the baby could clearly be seen holding the umbilical cord in its left hand, index finger raised, about to tap-taaap-tap.

On the way home Rebecca stopped at Waterstones and bought a guide to Morse Code. She spent the afternoon deciphering messages from her unborn child and tapping replies onto her tummy. She thought about asking the baby if he or she was a boy or a girl, but didn't.

Tony didn't ask about the scan, so Rebecca didn't tell him. She hid the Morse Code book in her knicker drawer and, at least when Tony was home, went about things as if nothing extraordinary was happening. Within a week or so she was familiar enough with Morse to manage conversations without the book. She would sit on the sofa, Tony in his armchair watching the footie, and tap away with the baby.

The pair talked about everything. Food was a favourite

and Rebecca would spend hours in the kitchen tasting different things, tapping names to the baby who would tap back likes and dislikes. They watched films together, Rebecca describing the stories and images in tap-taaaps, the baby asking all kinds of questions. What's a car? What are colours? What is love?

There was a time that Rebecca couldn't have answered that last one, she wouldn't have had the words, but now she gave her answer in Morse. *Taaap tap taaap taaap. Taaap taaap taaap. Tap Tap taaap.* Pause. *Tap taaap. Tap taaap tap. Tap.*

'You are,' she told her baby. Over and over again.

ULTRASOUND II

Huddled in the amniotic hush, the twins whispered to each other. Sensing the boy's furrowed brow through the fluid, the girl unfolded a hand and stroked his shin.

'Don't worry, little brother,' she said.

'But why can't it stay just us?'

The girl gamboled round, maneuvering the weight of her head to face her brother.

'It's how it happens for everyone,' she said.

She held her arms open and he floated into them. They held each other and listened. Outside the smothered voices of their parents could be heard, a muffle of sound with little meaning.

'They sound nice,' the girl said.

The boy nodded and she thought he might be crying, his shoulders shaking every now and then as they listened.

'Will we get to see them today?' said the boy.

'Yes, brother.'

'What do you think they'll look like?'

'Like us I suppose, only bigger.'

They had been told all about parents in their orientation, the stories that had somehow floated back to where they had been before here. No one back where they came from had ever seen a parent though, so it was hard for the twins to visualise one.

'That's the magic of these scans,' the girl said. 'We get to see them early. Time was a baby would have to wait until after the journey finished.'

'What if they don't like us?'

The girl took her brother's head in her hands and planted a kiss on his forehead.

'How could they not like you, my beautiful little brother?'

'Ewww,' said the boy, wiping the kiss off with the back of his hand but smiling as he did so.

'That's more like it,' the girl said.

They both felt the cold that told them the scan was starting. The boy kicked a foot out at the area of dark the sensation spread from.

'Stop that,' the girl said.

With closed eyes they followed the delicate pressure roaming across the skin standing between them and the wide world.

'There,' they whispered together as the sound curved around them, somehow forming a picture.

In front of them, two beaming faces fuzzed in and out of focus. They caught glimpses of smiles and eyes and curves of noses that reminded them of each other yet were somehow strange, alien.

'He has your eyes,' the girl said to her little brother.

'She has your smile,' the boy said to his big sister.

They held hands, smiling, as the faces washed in and out of view.

ULTRASOUND III

At seventeen weeks, Fran and Simon went private for the newest 3D-ultrasound. The ULED screen swirled with a milky colouring the texture of churning cream, the doctor angling it so Fran could see from the examination bed. The weight of the disc sensor pressed to the base of her bump emphasised the cold of the conductive gel.

'Remember, this will be unlike any regular scan. This is experimental technology.'

Simon squeezed Fran's hand as the image on the milky screen whisked itself into their baby.

'That's the baby's back.' The doctor pointed at the trail of tiny spinal bones running across the screen, then adjusted the position of the sensor slightly, sliding it across the slope of Fran's bump. 'There you are.'

Fran and Simon looked from the screen to each other and back to the screen as the face of their unborn child emerged from the swirl.

'Now for the clever part.'

The doctor pulled a second device, larger than the first and glowing at its end with a pale green light, from a holster moulded into the plastic chassis of the scanning unit. Squirting more conductive gel, he swept Fran's belly with the new device, swishing back and forth with the regularity of a windscreen wiper.

'And we are 3D,' the doctor said.

The baby curled from the screen, milk white and puffy round the edges as if made from scoops of ice-cream. Baby measured almost 13 centimetres long, about the size of a pear.

'Can I?' Fran reached out to her baby.

The doctor nodded and angled the screen down. Fran ran her fingers around her baby and pulled her to her chest with one hand, backhanding tears from her already-filled eyes with the other. Simon leaned in to stroke a finger down a fluffy white cheek.

'So warm,' he said.

'Perfect,' Fran said.

'Perfect,' they both said.

Fran lost her baby for the first time at 19 weeks. It was no one's fault. The doppler revealed no baby heartbeat during a routine appointment. A conventional ultrasound showed no movement. Fran delivered the baby the next day, a girl. She and Simon took turns holding her in the silent delivery room. Baby measured a little over 15 centimetres from crown to rump, about the size of a mango.

Simon waited until after the memorial service to set up the new TV and HDMI DVD player, putting it all together while Fran slept. When finally she came downstairs he told her all about the specifications of the TV, a set recommended by the 3D-ultrasound doctor. Fran just stared at the blank screen and waited.

'Are you ready?' Simon asked, checking the cable connections once more.

'Show me my baby,' Fran said.

As the baby churned and unfolded from the screen, Fran hunched over her daughter, wrapped her arms around all that remained of her and wept. Simon left the room to make some tea.

For nearly six months Fran did nothing but play the recording of her baby. Simon returned to work and Fran's mother watched over her, saw that she showered and remembered to eat. Fran refused to go out, barely spoke except to the projection of her baby.

Simon was home alone with Fran when she lost her baby a second time. He ran her a bath and herded her into it, then crept downstairs. The baby floated from the screen, wriggling as it slept and Simon stepped to her, knelt and took her in his arms. He held her until the sound of the bath being drained made its way downstairs, then kissed his daughter on her tiny forehead and let her go with a click of the TV's off switch.

He deleted the video files first, those on the PC and the backups on the terabyte drive, before removing the DVD and snapping it in two. He snatched a heavy glass tumbler from the kitchen and hurled it at the TV.

'What was that?' Fran called out on her way down the stairs.

She hesitated at the lounge door, taking in the cracked web of the screen, the pieces of DVD shining on the carpet, the shallow breathing of her husband sat on the sofa, head curled into his own lap. Eventually she realised she was screaming and threw herself upon Simon, raining fists down upon the back of his head.

WHAT WE DON'T TALK ABOUT WHEN WE TALK ABOUT CANCER

Liz is already holding my hand when the consultant enters. She squeezes hard, as if I'm falling and she might save me if she holds on hard enough. Mr Harlan stands on the other side of the bed from Liz, looks at me, then her, then me, then her, as he runs through my results.

Eventually he says, 'I really am very sorry.'

I nod.

Liz says, 'Surely there's something?'

There's a silence. The question rises like a balloon, until out of reach.

'When can I go home?'

'Tomorrow, all being well.'

With that Mr Harlan lifts my notes, taps the base of the folder on the tray table beside my bed. 'I'll be back to see you in the morning,' he says.

I nod.

At the door he stops, seems about to say something, but then doesn't.

Liz slides onto the bed. Careful to put no weight on me she huddles into my good side as best she can, pressing herself against me like a cat. She trembles with tiny sobs. I want to stroke her hair, but moving my arm that far would hurt too much, so I roll my head towards hers, rest my lips on her forehead. She smells of vanilla.

For a moment I think she might say it. I almost feel her think it. But we both say nothing.

Instead it is my cancer that speaks, its voice without malice. It sounds, if anything, almost sorry.

'Told you,' it says.

My cancer first spoke to me halfway through my initial round of chemo. I was alone in my hospital room trying to watch TV.

'I'm still here,' it said.

It spoke with a warm, ruffled drawl that told of too many cigarettes. A voice like my father's. I looked from the telly to the door, the voice so present I half-expected to see him stood there.

'In here,' the voice said.

I muted the TV.

'This isn't funny,' I called out to the empty room.

'No, it isn't,' said the voice.

I tried to stand but felt too sick, too dizzy to manage more than a small lift from my chair before collapsing back.

'It's okay,' it said. 'Relax.'

'Who is this? Who's there?'

I bellowed the questions. The voice did not reply.

'Is everything okay?'

One of the nurses stood at the door. She marched in and began checking my chemo drip.

'Was there someone outside?' I asked.

'You expecting somebody?'

Her eyes searched my face.

'Must have drifted off,' I said, 'Bad dream.'

'Okay then. Back in a minute,' she said.

The voice waited for her to finish changing the IV and leave before it spoke again.

'I really wouldn't start shouting. They'll be calling the men in white coats.'

I was quiet for a minute, listened to the steady beep of the chemo shunting into my veins.

'What are you?' I asked the voice.

The voice did not so much speak as appear, fully formed, in my head.

'You know what I am,' it said.

After we leave the hospital for the last time, my cancer doesn't speak for a while. Too many people around, too much going on. The kids come home as soon as Liz calls them. We have a houseful again. Liz bought one of those baby monitors so whoever's on Dad-duty in the night will hear me if I call. The kids are going to help Liz get a half-decent night's sleep.

I think myself lucky. That might sound funny, considering, but look at what I have. A beautiful wife, two gorgeous daughters, a strapping son. I've seen my eldest girl married, been given a beautiful granddaughter, been given time to watch her grow for three years. It's not like one minute I was diagnosed, the next I was dying. I've had four or five years of operations, radio-therapy, chemo, four or five years of sickness, of recuperation from surgery, of remission followed by renewed activity, of pissing in a bag, of eventually shitting in a bag. Just lying here is an exercise in finding the least excruciating of a multitude of agonising positions, and I'm sipping spoon after spoon of morphine just to reduce the pain to an irritating hum. I'm not saying any of this has been easy, it's just that, here, listening to the sound of them downstairs, I can only think of what I would have missed if I hadn't made it through all that bollocks.

I'll be hooked up soon. Doctor Khan signed off on the morphine drip when he was here earlier. He said I'd likely slip into a coma and that would be that. Liz gripped my hand like she always does. I didn't tell her I'm glad. That right, now that's all I want. To crawl out from under this rotten body.

Everyone's downstairs. I told them I needed to sleep after Doctor Khan left. I can hear them all, doing their best to be quiet, but it's impossible with a houseful. Liz is clanking pots in the kitchen, busying herself making lunch for them all. I know she's glad of the distraction: the voices, the intermittent and fragile laughter, the tiny stomp of my granddaughter on the kitchen tiles. It's the sound of what life will be like once I have gone. It is hushed right now, but will strengthen with time. I lie still and listen and my cancer finally has something to say.

'Not long now,' it whispers to me.

'Good,' I say.

'You asked for this.'

'And I'm grateful, but enough's enough.'

We listen to the noise from downstairs, a murmur of voices punctuated by my grandaughter's squealing laughter. The sound of life going on.

'I'm ready,' I say, eventually.

From the beginning I made deals with it. 'Let me give Jenny away, let me have that,' I asked it after they fitted the first stoma. I walked my eldest girl down the aisle, terrified my urostomy would leak. After that it was, 'Let me see my granddaughter.' This one whispered as I lay in my hospital bed, waiting for morning and the op to fit my colostomy. I asked for more and more as time went on and each time my cancer answered with the question.

'Are you sure?'

'Yes,' I whispered each time.

'I'll give you what you want, but I'll need a little more of you in return.'

I nodded each time.

It clawed at my bladder, ate chunks of my bowel, sucked on my body weight, gargled my blood. At times it left me half dead. There are photos, the kids' graduations, Jenny's wedding, family holidays, Lisa's christening, where I look like a punctured inflatable of myself, half the air already escaped. But I'm smiling. In every photo you can see I'm still smiling.

'You should say your goodbyes,' Doctor Khan says.

I smile at Liz. 'We've been saying goodbye for four years now,' I say looking at her.

The kids come up one at a time and kiss me and take turns lying for a bit on Liz's side of the bed. They are careful not to hold too tight. I tell them to be good. To look after their mother. To look out for each other. When they get upset I tell them not to worry about me. In a little while it will be over. They've got the hard bit. They have to pick themselves up and carry on. All I have to do now is die.

I don't say that last bit out loud, but it hangs in the air each time I say goodbye to each of my beautiful children.

Last to see me is my lovely Lisa, the grandest of grand-daughters. There was some argument over whether she should be allowed to see me like this. Until Lisa stomped her foot and demanded in the way only a three-year-old can. She's totally unafraid when she comes in and clambers onto the bed. Jenny is at the door, watching her fierce little girl.

'Mummy says I mustn't hurt you, Grandy,' Lisa chirps.

I lean my head up off my pile of pillows and skim my lips on her forehead.

'You could never hurt me, pickle,' I say, 'You're too lovely to hurt me.'

For a moment No Tears shampoo, strawberry yoghurt on her sweetly sour breath, and the last faint remnants of her baby smell overwhelm the gamy air of the room.

She nestles in beside me and begins to sing. *I can sing a rainbow*. Her voice is soft and sweet and delicate. I cling to it.

'Beautiful, beautiful,' is all I can say, over and over, when she finishes.

'My birthday party coming, Grandy. I wear my princess dress.' I look over to Jenny and see her face crumble a little. 'You come to my party, Grandy?' Lisa says. 'We do dancing.' She grins and laughs and does a little shuffle where she sits.

'Careful of Grandy, sweetheart.' Jenny, wiping her eyes with her sleeve, takes a step forward, but I wave her back.

'She's all right.'

'See,' Lisa says to her mother, then sticks out her tongue and blows a delicious raspberry, tripping into laughter at the end. Jenny frowns and Lisa turns to me. I chuckle with her and she laughs even more. When I look back to Jenny, she is laughing too.

'You be good for your mummy now,' I say to Lisa.

She nods. 'I'm a good girl,' she says.

'Yes, you are. You're good, you're clever-clever and you're Grandy's beautiful girl.'

I tell her this over and over, hoping to glimpse her memory of my saying it form behind her eyes, but I'm out of time. The nurse is outside. They're ready. Lisa stands at the door and waves at me with both hands like she's off home. Like she'll see me tomorrow.

'Bye bye, Grandy," she says

'Bye bye, little pickle,' I manage, tears smudging my last look at her.

Liz comes in and holds me as the nurse hooks me up.

'I love you,' she says. I can see her eyes searching for something less clichéd, something less obvious.

'We've already said it all,' I say and her hand sits in my hand like it has always been there, like it will always be there.

The machine starts its steady tick and hiss and beep and a lead wave of morphine breaks over me, the first of a tide that will sweep in and carry me away. There is only one thing I need to hear now. I close my eyes and wait.

Drifting in and out, I talk with my cancer.

'One more deal,' I say. My words slur and I stumble even over these few, but it understands. It always understands.

'Just one,' it says, ' there's only time for one.'

'Let me stay to hear it.'

My cancer is quiet for a long time. I see blurs of Liz and the kids moving around me. Snatches of their conversations reach me, sounds from a far-off shore, receding, wave by wave, receding.

'You're sure?' my cancer asks, finally.

I nod.

After this there are no more words. The pain, like a seabed, is drowned under the morphine wash of my thoughts. I feel Liz sat beside me on the bed, sense the kids in the room, close. My youngest has my other hand. In this way I wait.

I know it is coming when Liz climbs up on the bed beside me. I feel her urgency. For months, for years she has been careful, something as simple as a proper cuddle made impossible by too many operations, by stomas and bags fixed to my flesh, by too much pain. Finally, she grabs me, pulls me to her. She can't hurt me. She knows she can't hurt me now. She knows she could never really hurt me. She never hurt me. She holds me to her and I feel my head on her breast I feel my head on her feel the skin of her feel her and slowly I have her voice on me in my ear around me her voice just hers everywhere else is silence and her voice is a hand holding me and she tells me it's all right she tells me you can go now she tells me you've done enough now she tells me rest, please rest she tells me please she tells me I love you she tells me you can go she tells me please she tells me I love you let go and it is not the pain that carries me away not the drugs it is not fear or anger or the voice I've carried round inside me for too long it is just the sound of her voice just the sound of her voice the sound of her voice sound of her voice of her voice

STORM IN A TEACUP

The cup is Alice Stout's. It is a simple, off-white thing, one of many to be found in the café she runs with husband, Sid. From outside comes the rumble of Bridgenorth's funicular railway, heralding the imminent arrival of the morning trade, but right now it is not quite opening time for The Tea Cosy, and Alice sits at one of the tables she has already laid. She gulps her tea, then stops still for just a moment or two, her elbows on the table, her hands wrapped around the cup. It is empty but for a thin layer of sweet milky tea coating the ceramic inside. This is how the storm begins, as if somehow the heat from Alice's hands warms the cup and, by conduction, the air inside.

It is important to note that there is nothing unusual about the cup itself. Today, this sunny morning in 1973, it is what is about to happen inside the cup that is unusual. A centre of low pressure surrounded by a system of high pressure is about to develop, which will result, when the opposing forces meet, in the creation of winds and storm clouds. Cumulonimbus. Literally, accumulated rain.

Even if the slowly emerging systems of the storm were visible, Alice would not see them. Her head is filled with 1951, specifically the summer of that year. In her pocket she has seven torn ticket stubs for the cliff railway. She has kept them, tucked away in the bottom of her jewellery box, for decades. She has not thought of them in years, yet this morning she woke and simply had to find them, tuck them safely into the pocket of her apron, bring them with her when she came down from the flat. Thoughts of the tickets crowd Alice's head while her hands inexplicably warm the cup she holds before her like a chalice.

The rumble from the cliff railway grows louder and shakes Alice from her thoughts. She crosses the café and places the cup down on the serving counter next to the till. Inside, the air churns and swirls. Differing pressures prepare to meet as Alice gets on with laying the tables.

In the crumpled row of buildings leading to the cliff railway in High Town, The Tea Cosy huddles between a dusty antique emporium and the grease-smeared shopfront of the local fish and chip shop. A faded sign swings above the door, the ghost of a painting. A teapot upon a tray, surrounded by cups and saucers, a milk jug, and a sugar bowl. The teapot in the picture wears what must once have been a colourful cosy, now grayed and faded; its yellows turned to mustard, its blues shifting to smoke, its reds barely pink, more the muddy brown of old tea stains. A sallow net curtain hangs in the window through which little can be seen from the outside.

Sid Stout, Alice's husband of just over twenty-five years if you count the summer of 1951, or just under if you don't, stands in the kitchen looking out through the hatch, watching Alice lay the café's seven circular tables. She looks good for her age. A much younger woman would be proud of the fall of her red hair and the way she fills her simple red dress and striped apron. It is her eyes that Sid is watching for though. Her eyes are green. He struggles for the right word. Emerald? Apple? Forest? He settles for sage, both the shade and the peppery flavour seem right for Alice. It strikes Sid that though the café they share is worn about the edges and, by his own admission, he himself is frayed with age, Alice still glows. But even as he takes pleasure at the way she moves about the room, the sense of unease, with him since he woke this morning, grows. This feeling, that he has forgotten something important, looms over him.

'What are you looking so glum for?' Alice asks. She is stood at the door to the café about to open up, and looks back at him with an exasperation that they both know is also love.

'Nothing.'

'Still love me?' she says, and Sid does not hesitate with his reply.

'Always.'

She smiles. 'Good. Now get back to work.'

And with that, Alice flips the sign hanging in the window from CLOSED to OPEN.

Miniature hot air currents climb the curve of the cup's tea-stained surface, cool air down drafts in the centre of the tiny space. It is still too soon to tell what form this particular storm will take, if there will be hail or thunder and lightning, whether it will be a rainstorm, a snowstorm, an ice storm, a tropical storm, or a hurricane, if it will cause flooding or wildfires. Forgotten by Alice as she darts back and forth from kitchen to café, unnoticed by Sid as he stirs and chops and warms oil in the kitchen, the cup sits on the faded Formica beside the till, the storm inside growing.

Tommy sits at his usual table, having scraped together enough coppers for a full English. It will be his last visit of the week to the Cosy, as payday is still three days away. He smokes a roll-up. The twine holding his trousers in place and fastening his jacket about him marks Tommy as a man in need of a wife. A pair of yarks band his knees, holding his trouser cuffs clear of the dried mud upon his work boots. His hat, a worn cap with a well-thumbed peak, sits on the table along with his tobacco pouch and cigarette papers.

Tommy is the only customer to have walked the cliff steps this morning, the funicular rail cars passing him at least twice as he clambered up the steep stone path. It was a choice between a ticket or breakfast, and when Alice brings out his eggs and bacon, he digs in, a grin bursting through his furiously bristling beard.

'Cheers, Alice,' he says.

'You're very welcome, Tommy love,' she replies, already walking away.

A fine woman, a real catch that one. Tommy smiles, imagining what it must be like to have such a woman for a wife. Egg yolk runs into the thatch of his beard and he wipes it away with a threadbare cuff. Tommy sees Sid watching from the kitchen hatch, unsure if he is looking at Alice or at Tommy himself. He reddens but no one notices, his flushed cheeks too well hidden under his thick beard. The only visible sign of his embarrassment is the sweat breaking on his forehead, but everyone knows Tommy walks the cliff steps each morning, reason enough for anyone to be sweating cobs.

Emily Blakemore sits at the table nearest the window, her terrier, Clarence, snuffling at her feet. Every now and then she twitches the smoke-yellowed net curtain up and scans the cobbles leading down to the cliff railway.

'He'll be along in a minute,' Alice says.

Emily drops the curtain as if stung. She hides her eyes by fixing them on the menu card and catches her breath.

'Tea and a crumpet?' Alice says.

The bell above the door jangles. The man entering wears a suit and overcoat, and his polished brogues snap on the worn linoleum. He crosses the café without a word and takes a seat at the table furthest from the other customers, his back to them.

'Tea and a crumpet, ta.'

As Emily speaks, her bosom heaving beneath her dress, her eyes lock on the shoulders of the man across the room. Alice nods and slips across to the smartly-dressed man. Emily smiles as he orders tea and a crumpet.

Clarence is the first to sense the developing storm, his ears leaping forward, furrowing the fur of his brow. The dog flicks his eyes this way, that way, their frantic movement emphasised in the stillness of his body. He hears a crumpling sound and turns to face it but cannot see inside the cup from where he is on the floor. The little dog looks to his owner, but Emily's eyes remain fixed on the back and shoulders of the suited man. The crumpling sound comes again, louder. It drags Clarence up on his paws, sends him scampering back and forth under the table.

'Clarence!' Emily barks at the dog and, obediently, he collapses back to the floor, his head on his paws. He hears the crumpling sound again and rolls his eyes once more up to his mistress, but she is watching the man again. Clarence stares dolefully at the ankles of the others, but they are all too busy with their food or their paper or each other. Clarence drops his eyes and whines.

The bell above the door rings again and a lad in jeans and a donkey jacket steps in. His face is straggled with long hair and a largely failed attempt at a beard. He sits at the table between Emily and the suited man, causing Emily to sigh. Her huffing has the lad, David, look to his left and right for the cause of the offence she is so obviously taking, but seeing nothing of note he collapses back in the chair.

'Coffee,' he says to Alice once she makes her way to him. 'Please.'

He has been awake much of the night, finally sleeping on a bench facing out over the sandstone cliffs, the rush of the Severn, one hundred feet below, reduced to an ambient lullaby. The rattle and hum of the funicular railway's first departure from High Town woke him. Before rising from the dew-damp bench, he sat, the river and Low Town before him, the cliff railway rattling along beside him, the castle ruins still sleeping behind him, and he watched the cliff rail cars leave and arrive, leave and arrive. Now, in the warmth of the café, he watches Alice take in his disheveled appearance.

'I can pay,' he says, pulling a handful of coins from his pocket.

'No, love, don't fret about that.' Alice smiles and points to the rear of the shop. 'You can use the basin out back to clean yourself up while I get your coffee.'

David nods, thanks her, and scuffs across the café and out the back.

'Oi!' shouts Sid as the young lad passes.

'Leave 'im be,' Alice calls through the kitchen hatch.

'Not another waif and stray,' Sid mutters loud enough for Alice to hear, then he smiles. 'You're a soft one, Alice Stout,' he says.

'Must be to stay married to you,' she calls back, and right

then her thoughts turn to the ticket stubs in her pocket. Something must show in her eyes because Sid stops sharp and, feeling suddenly tense but unable to say why, watches after her as she turns to see to the boy's coffee.

Cyril, sits at the table nearest the kitchen and sips his tea. Between every other sip he checks the time on his wrist-watch as if the act of his drinking were somehow part of the device's workings. A newspaper rests on the table before him. He glances at the open pages, running his hand through his receding, close-cropped hair. He checks his watch again, this time holding it up to his ear, searching for the tick and tock and tick of it. Satisfied that time is moving as it should be, he half turns. Somewhere in the corner of his vision he is aware of someone watching him, and he swings his head the other way to better take in whoever it is.

His eyes lock upon the woman with the dog at the table nearest the café window. He recognises her from the library. They have spoken once or twice as she stamped his books, but he only knows her by her surname. She stares across at him and he back at her and he grows suddenly clammy. Feeling his face flush, he yanks a handkerchief from his breast pocket, covers both palms with the white cotton, and sweeps it over his face and up to his diminished hairline. The upward action leaves what little remains of his fringe sticking up like a poorly-pruned bush. Folding the sweat-damp handkerchief, he glances across once more to find her still looking, and he turns hurriedly back to his tea. He takes a sip, checks his watch, takes another sip. When he turns in his seat once more, the scruffy boy is back at his table, and Cyril's view is blocked.

~

A supercell thunderstorm is characterized by the presence of a deep, rotating updraft or mesocyclone forming
as strong changes of wind speed or direction set part of
the lower atmosphere spinning in invisible, tube-like rolls.
Supercells are often isolated from other rainstorms and,
most importantly, can be any size. The one forming in the
cup is picking up speed. The first rumbles of its churning
clouds are too quiet for any but Clarence to hear. The cup
sits where it has been left, the magnificent event taking
place inside it unnoticed by the Cosy's proprietors and
patrons alike. The storm clouds brew and swirl like malig-
nant cappuccino froth.

Outside The Tea Cosy, a blue sky promises much for the
day. A few shapes hurry past the window, folk on their way
to wherever, lacking the time for a cup of tea or a need for
breakfast, oblivious to the extraordinary nature of what is
about to happen inside.

The coffee is bitter and makes David wince with each sip,
but the heat of it begins to revive his spirits. He wraps his
fingers round the cup, warming his hands along with his
insides. Looking up, he sees the waitress watching him. She
smiles and he smiles back, mouthing a thank you for the
use of the washstand as much as the coffee.

Placing his cup down upon its saucer, he checks his
pocket. The jingle of coins is reassuring, and he does not
feel the need to count them. The weight and sound are
heavy enough to assure him he has the cash to pay for his
drink, a ride to Low Town on the funicular railway, and a
bus to work from the stop below.

Perhaps he will try Liz from the phone box on the way, if

he can think of what to say. Sipping once more at his coffee, fingers wrapped once more around the cup, he mulls over how to fix things with a girl who no longer loves him.

Everyone for the moment served, Alice steps back into the kitchen and walks to where Sid stands washing-up, his back to her. She steps close in to him, slipping her arms under his, wrapping them about his chest. She rests her head for a moment on his back at the place where his neck and shoulders meet. Her hands slide inside his shirt and rest between the fabric of his vest and shirt as if between bedsheets. He turns his head toward her, and she tips her toes and lifts her lips to meet his cheek. Sid smiles, a fag balanced between his lips.

'What's that for?'
'For being here.'
Something they always say.
Her head fills with thoughts of the tickets and what they mean. His head dizzies with another rush of unease. Sid turns his face back to the soapy water of the sink, and Alice slips from him like she's stepping out of a dress. At that exact moment a shriek fills the near silence of the café.

Everyone is on their feet and looking at the counter. Light flashes and cracks from within the teacup. It trembles imperceptibly with the tiny power of the storm inside. Emily shrieks again. Clarence yaps at her feet and then begins to stalk toward the storm-filled teacup, his growls an unending curl of consonants. The storm cloud answers with a rumble that sends the terrier skittering back to the feet of his owner, yelping.

'How is it the cup ain't moving?' Sid leans in, staring hard at the churning thunderhead. He purses his lips then blows a blast of air at the cup, and the cloud ruffles, spiraling with the updraft from within. Sid, growing more obfuscated as the clouds darken, raises a hand to the cup.

'Sid, what're you doing?'

'Calm down, Alice love. Just gonna give it a little poke.'

Pointing a tobacco-stained finger at the dense cauliflower blossoms of cloud, he inches it forward, hesitates, then dabs it in. A flash and crack echo on the walls of the café.

'Bleedin' hell!' he bellows and whips his finger out. The end is black and smoking and he blows on it for a second or two before plunging it into his mouth.

'Sid, language.'

'Hmmmit bleeeebiin yuuurts,' Sid groans through the finger clenched in his cheek.

They have made a horseshoe around the cup, all except for Clarence, who lies whining beneath a table. Cyril squats, his eyes level with the cup, watching intently. 'There,' he says, 'see that?'

A tiny flash, like the spark of a flint lighter, illuminates the cloud from beneath. A roll of thunder follows, a sound like fingers tapping on a table top.

'A proper storm then, lightning and everything,' Cyril says, a surprised chuckle shaking him for a second. 'Remarkable.'

No one speaks for a time, mesmerised by the adumbrating swirl of air. They lean in as one, lulled to silence and stillness by the tiny ferocity of the wind escaping the cup and, together, they begin to see.

For Alice it is her love for Sid she sees twisting itself inside and out, a dense cloud of emotion that rolls and thunders. It is the love that had her say nothing when she found, all those years ago, Sid had been 'taking tea' with

Reeny Moseley from Low Town. He was seen and word got back to Alice, but she never spoke of it. Before the gossip found its way to her ear, she knew he'd been up to something because she found the ripped ticket stubs for the cliff railway in the pocket of his trousers. Always one ticket. Not the two half stubs still joined that she put in her purse as they made their way home from The Black Boy Inn down on the Cartway on a Friday night. Love held her tongue though, long enough for the single stubs to stop appearing. He stopped going and that was all she needed to know. But she kept the tickets. There were seven. They marked the number of visits her Sid made to Reeny Mosley. Alice sees all this in the turn of the tiny storm, and her hand reaches into her pocket.

David pushes his fringe from his face. 'It's beautiful,' he says. It is Liz's face that forms, for just a fraction, in the clouds and mouths the memory of her words, spoken just the night before, words that sent David wandering the streets of High Town long after the last bus carried her home, words that left him sleeping on a bench. As the cloud-face mutely shapes the words, David speaks them aloud. 'I don't want to see you anymore,' he says, and like that the face is gone as quick as it takes to tell – quicker – and the storm turns and David smiles once more at the tiny beauty of it. Already beginning to forget Liz Layton, his thoughts turn to other girls.

At the same time, Emily speaks. 'A miracle,' she says, the words muffled by the hand covering her mouth. To her the roil of the cloud is the energy and flare of feelings she has kept too long locked up within her chest, her form forced to quake with unexpressed longing. Emily Blakemore, librarian and spinster, has watched Cyril Renshaw from afar for many years, her feelings for him buttoned tight inside her like a child's treasure in a secret pocket. If one were to check her borrowing history against that of Mr. Renshaw, it would show she is long in the habit of borrowing each of his selections upon their return to the library. Each book Cyril borrows he decorates with marginalia, his thoughts scribbled with HB pencil in the white space of each page. Emily, taking the books home, pours over his comments, rubbing them from page after page to save him the fine. She writes the best of his thoughts down in her diary, replies to them in ink on bound paper, scripting imagined conversations in the soft light of her reading lamp, knowing that speaking to him would really be the most impossible thing in the world. It takes the turn of the storm to move her eyes to Cyril's. He too has seen her love for him in the motion of it, and he returns her gaze. Her knees buckle. She gasps and staggers to a chair, Clarence leaping to her lap as she lands on the seat.

'Are you all right, Miss?' Cyril asks, stepping to her with eager concern.

'I . . . it . . . I . . . yes,' Emily squeaks, her eyes wide and darting as a hare's.

With all eyes on Emily, no one notices the colour drain from Sid's face or hears him whisper to himself, 'Bloody fool,' as he stares into the dark insides of the clouds. There he sees just how much he loves his wife, and each thunderclap is a reprimand. He is surprised to find he has forgotten the name of the woman. He didn't expect that, to forget someone who had once seemed so important. He thinks how lucky he is Alice never found out just where it was he slipped out to those Saturday afternoons in the summer of '51. He never thinks of those moments, but he is thinking of them now, watching the storm. Inside Sid, a low pressure of gratitude meets a high pressure of relief, and his heart thunders at the sordid stupidity of his younger self.

'That thing ain't right,' Sid bellows. He marches into the kitchen returning with the heavy fireplace tongs, waving them in front of him like a toy sword.

'Sidney Stout, what in giddy goodness do you think you're doing?' Alice says, stepping into his path. 'You leave it be for a minute.'

'Quite right,' Cyril says and places himself alongside Alice, between the cup and Sid.

'That thing ain't natural!' Sid shouts, trying to sidestep the pair.

'I must insist you stop.' Cyril moves to once more block Sid's approach.

'This is my café, so it's my say so.' Sid waves the tongs in Cyril's face. 'Get out me way or I'll wrap these round your noggin.'

'Sidney Stout.'

Cyril takes a step to Sid. Their heated breath mingles in the air where their cold stares meet.

'You desperate for a beltin'?' Sid waggles the tongs at Cyril once more, his head pecking back and forth like a furious pigeon, but Alice steps in and yanks them from his hand.

'You daft apeth, give me those.'

Sid squeals as Alice takes his ear in her fist and pulls him toward the kitchen.

'Your café, is it? Do as you please, will you, Sidney Stout?'

'Alice, let me loose right now,' he blusters, which only makes her twist all the harder.

Cyril turns to find Emily standing beside him, gazing at him as if he's just fought off a lion.

'Don't let him fluster you, Mr. Renshaw,' she says, her

face puffed with admiration. 'Violence is the desperate act of the fearful, the cowardly, the uncivilised.'

Cyril recognises the words as his own scribbled, marginalised thoughts. His head is a flurry of confused realisation, and Emily, in a moment of unforeseen bravery, takes his hand in hers.

'Miss Blakemore?'

Cyril watches her smile. He has not seen her do this in all his visits to the library, their brief, blurted conversations punctuated instead by the thump of the date stamp.

'Mr. Renshaw.'

And the flush of feeling bursts about them both, pulsing with the rising shouts of Sid and Alice in the kitchen and the call and reply of the lightning and thunder bouncing out of the cup.

None of the others notice Tommy pull up a chair and seat himself next to the counter, his eyes level with the cup. The furious churn of the storm grips him. He hears a hurried tinkling as tiny fists of hail sugar the bottom of the cup. For the first time in years he does not think of Alice. The storm's rumble elongates, thunder and lightening overlapping. A tinny crescendo rattles inside the ceramic shelter of the cup. Tommy looks about the café as he rolls himself a fag. The suit and the wallflower lean into each other, gripped in some picture-house fantasy of love. The young lad sits back at his table, drinking the last of his coffee, a stupid grin upon his face. The shouting from the kitchen rolls along, fuelled by years of the same air rolling about the system, throwing up the same arguments and the same passions, the same lows and highs.

Tommy thinks of the low pressure deep inside him, heated by years of watching Alice with Sid. Feeling the storm inside him building, his eyes rest back upon the teacup, and he tucks the finished roll-up behind his ear for later. Lightning illuminates his face like a lightbulb filament overpowered by a surge of electricity: a flash and then blackness. Tommy doesn't think at this point. He simply raises the cup to his lips and drinks down the storm, rain and hail and all. Cloud moustaches his top lip. A ragged fork of lightning numbs his tongue, filling his mouth with the taste of metal.

A silence falls over the café and all heads turn to him as Tommy drains the last of the storm from the teacup. He licks his lips, wipes them with the back of his hand to remove the last of the cloud.

'What did it taste like?'

It is Alice who asks. Tommy stands mute for a moment then burps, an invisible cloud of ionized air spreading from him, charged like the sky after a storm.

'Like falling in and out of love,' he says.

They sit around a table, all eyes on the once more empty and unremarkable teacup placed in the middle. The atmosphere, the hush, the shared quiet, is fresh and speaks of change and clear skies and new beginnings.

Cyril and Emily hold hands beneath the table, fingers wrapping and unwrapping each other as if checking and rechecking they are still there.

Alice thumbs the ticket stubs in the pocket of her apron, rolls each one into a tight ball.

David runs his fingers through his hair, pushes his fringe from his eyes, still smiling.

Sid breathes deeply and, pulling Alice's hand from her pocket, he holds it tight.

The storm winds through the complicated path of

Tommy's digestive system, the cold simplicity of it over-whelming the frazzling heat of his unrequited love. He picks up the cup from the table, slips it into the pocket of his tattered jacket and, taking the roll-up from behind his ear and lighting it, leaves without a word. He will not think of Alice at all when, later, he remembers back to the day he swallowed a storm.

Sid strokes the back of Alice's hand with his thumb and she turns to him.

David's eyes close, and his head folds into his arms on the table. He dozes in the sun that beats through the yellowed net across the café window.

Alice whispers, 'Still love me?' in Sid's ear. She knows his reply before he gives it.

Cyril and Emily, still holding hands, slip out into the day going on outside. He will walk her to the library this morning, though it is not on his way to work. This evening he will select six books and wait for the library to close, then walk her home.

Sid moves back to the kitchen, but not before pulling Alice to him. Their kiss feels, to both of them, like the old days. For just a moment their lips, if not the rest of them, are young again and innocent.

Alice waits until Sid is back at the sink before she begins to clear the tables. She scrapes leftovers from butter-smeared plates. Looking up, to be sure Sid is not watching, she takes the balled-up ticket stubs from her pocket and, one by one, drops them into the bin.

ACKNOWLEDGEMENTS

To Nicholas Royle, who gave this still emerging writer a much-needed confidence boost at just the right time.

To Jodi Cleghorn, Sara Crowley and Neil Baker, for reading my stories and telling me when I'm going wrong.

To Andy Othling whose music as Lowercase Noises accompanied much of the writing contained in these covers, providing the perfect soundtrack to my fictional world.

To my parents, who showed me the joy of reading and said I'd be published one day.

To my kids, who make me a better writer, father, person everyday.

And to Susie, without whom I would not make sense.

I would also like to thank the editors of the following publications where stories in this collection first appeared:

'Looking Out of Broken Windows' was first published in Paraxis (2012); 'Half-mown Lawn won the Yeovil Literary Prize for short fiction (2010), was first published by Ether

Books on the Ether app (2011) and was later included in Salt Publishing's *The Best British Short Stories 2012*; 'Baggage,' 'Ultrasounds,' and 'Leaving What's Left' were published on *Metazen* (2010, 2010 & 2011); 'Connecting' was published in issue 35 of *The View From Here* (2011); 'Impact' was published in the charity anthology *100 Stories for Haiti* (2010); 'Strutting and Fretting' appeared on the National Flash Fiction Day Flashes website as part of the NFFD 2012 celebrations; an earlier version of 'Did You Pack This Bag Yourself?' was published in eMergent Publishing's anthology *The Yin and Yang Book* under the title 'This Be The Verse' (2010); 'What Precise Moment' was published in *Eclectic Flash* (2010); 'Soiled' was featured in the online literary journal *Friction* (2012); 'The Man Who Lived Like A Tree' was published by Referential and was nominated for a Best of The Net Award and a Pushcart Prize (2012); 'Things I No Longer Wish To Possess' was published by Staccato (2011); 'Third Party, Fire & Theft' was published in issue 25 of *Neon* (2011), and 'Storm in a Teacup' won a *Carve* Esoteric Award in 2013 and was published in the Spring 2013 edition of *Carve Magazine*.